DENNIS PIERCE

Cross Checking

A Parker Hanson Mystery

I

Blind Hate

Chapter 1

"Let me get this straight. You want to hire me for a *treasure hunt?*"

I was sitting at a table in the Tipsy Moose, an upscale bar in Manchester, New Hampshire. The Tipsy Moose was where my downstairs neighbor, Amalia Velasquez, tended bar five days a week. It was also where I'd begun meeting clients for my private investigator business lately, a step up in class from the Starbucks on Route 28 that used to serve as my makeshift office space.

It was late September, and the Bruins were playing a preseason game on the television screens scattered around the bar. The Red Sox had fallen out of playoff contention by mid-August, and no one was paying attention to them anymore.

The man sitting opposite me was tall and thin, with neatly trimmed, curly hair the color of flax seed. His name was Peter Bowles, and he owned an estate sale company based in Nashua.

I must have spoken these words to Bowles a little too loudly, because half the people in the bar turned to look at me. But he barely reacted to my incredulity. Judging from his demeanor, he must have thought it was the most natural thing in the world to have asked for my help in finding a hidden fortune.

He leaned in and nodded gravely. "Yes, that's right."

Bowles wore a herringbone-patterned brown tweed blazer with a blue cashmere sweater underneath. His overcoat was draped over the chair behind him, but he was still wearing his maroon wool scarf indoors.

He reached into the inside breast pocket of his blazer and pulled out a small, leather-bound journal.

"I found this in the bottom drawer of an antique rolltop desk that was part of the estate for a man named Walter Cobb," he said with an air of solemnity, placing the book down on the table in front of me. "Cobb passed away unexpectedly earlier this month at the age of sixty-eight. He came from an enormously wealthy family in Bedford. But he never married, and his only living relative is a niece who lives in Amherst. Her name is Cynthia Forrest."

His voice barely rising above a whisper, Bowles continued: "Ms. Forrest hired me to liquidate her uncle's estate. I discovered this journal as I was going through his possessions, and I asked her if she wanted to keep it for sentimental reasons. When she said no, I began reading it to see if it contained any information of cultural or historical significance, which might give it some value in an estate sale. I didn't find anything like that, but I did come across these highlighted passages."

While Bowles was thumbing through the journal, I stole a quick glance at one of the TV screens. The Bruins were leading the Washington Capitals, 1-0, midway through the first period.

Bowles found the page he was looking for and handed the journal to me. I read the words he'd highlighted with a faded yellow marker:

June 3, 1990—
Acquired a priceless treasure today.

Its nature is so sensitive that I dare not describe it.
I'll have to devise a way to stow it away secretly.

He took the book from me, flipped ahead a few pages, and handed it back. The words he'd highlighted on this new page read:

> *August 27, 1990—*
> *Stashed treasure from Romeo Hotel, Lima, with Beth/Meredith.*
> *Key in C.*
> *Corner lot, November 15.*

As I looked up from the journal, Bowles met my gaze with a triumphant grin. "See? Cobb not only refers to a priceless treasure, but he's also given us a clue to its location."

Just three months earlier, Amalia and I had exposed a gun smuggling operation with ties to New Hampshire Governor Jack Gordon's administration. The case had brought a lot of prestige to my private investigator business, and I'd been fielding many requests for my services since then. Not surprisingly, this spike in business included a number of unconventional requests as well as traditional ones.

But this was definitely one of the strangest.

"Mr. Bowles, I appreciate that you thought of me. But I have to say, I'm highly skeptical. How do we know this journal is authentic? How can we be sure these aren't just the ramblings of a guy who's losing his grip on reality? Hell, maybe Mr. Cobb was simply jotting down notes for a novel he was writing."

Bowles made a tent with his fingers in front of his face before responding.

"Mr. Hanson, I understand your skepticism. But I checked with Cynthia Forrest, and she confirms this is her uncle's handwriting. As for whether there really is a treasure, that's what I'm hoping *you* can determine."

He continued: "Walter Cobb was a collector of rare artifacts from around the world, and he used this journal to describe the items he'd obtained and where they came from. I've compared the other entries in this journal with the list of Cobb's possessions, and he kept a remarkably accurate record of his purchases. This tells me Cobb wasn't a man prone to exaggeration or flights of fancy. On the contrary, he was meticulous and systematic by nature. I think he was telling the truth when he made those entries in his journal. And besides, where's the harm in pursuing this matter? It seems to me like it's a fairly low risk, in return for the chance at a pretty hefty reward."

A collective groan swept through the bar, and I used my highly attuned deductive reasoning skills to figure out the Caps had just scored to tie the hockey game at one goal apiece.

"Okay," I said after a few moments of thought. "I charge sixty dollars an hour, plus expenses. I'll dig around, see what I can learn about the existence of this 'treasure' you think Cobb has stashed away. But I have to warn you, there's not a lot to go on here. I don't know how successful I'm going to be."

"I'll pay you a full week's salary just to see what you can learn," Bowles said. "If you haven't come up with anything by the end of a week, I'll cut my losses. But as an added incentive, if there *is* a treasure and you're able to find it, I'll give you forty percent of whatever my share is."

My eyes grew wide. "And where does Ms. Forrest fit into the picture?"

"In return for selling off her uncle's estate, I keep forty percent of all the proceeds I generate for her," Bowles replied. "As Cobb's sole heir, whatever fortune we might find would pass on to her, minus my forty-percent commission."

I did a quick mental calculation. Forty percent of forty percent was sixteen percent. That meant I stood to receive sixteen percent of whatever the total value of Cobb's hidden "treasure" might be.

But sixteen percent of *what*? It could be untold millions … or I could simply be hunting for snipe.

I felt a little foolish for agreeing, but I told Bowles we had a deal and that I would send him a contract in the morning. As we stood and shook hands, one more question occurred to me.

"How do you know I can be trusted to hand over this so-called 'treasure' to you if I do manage to find it?"

He looked me in the eyes and smiled. "Mr. Hanson, I've done my homework, and I'm confident I can trust you. Why do you think I came to you in the first place?"

* * *

When Bowles left the Tipsy Moose, I joined Amalia's girlfriend, Kris Koskinen, at the bar. Every time I saw Kris, she was fashionably dressed. On this occasion, she was wearing a black belted dress with a Mandarin-style collar. Her blonde hair was swept up in a pony tail.

"So you're looking for buried treasure now?" she teased me as I sat on a stool next to her. "Do you have a map and everything?"

"Oh, you overheard? Yeah, I don't know what this guy expects me to find, but I doubt anything will come from it."

"Well, if you *do* discover a hidden fortune, maybe Nicolas

Cage will play you in the movie version someday."

"Hmmph. More like Steve Buscemi."

Amalia was working behind the bar, and she greeted me with a fist bump. "*Hola*, neighbor. Want a beer?"

"Yes, please."

Nine months after undergoing triple bypass surgery, I was trying to stick to a healthy diet, and I was still avoiding alcohol. But Amalia had introduced me to this incredible, game-changing IPA from Athletic Brewing Company, called Run Wild. It tasted just like a craft-brewed IPA, but without the stuff that gives you a nice buzz—while also pummeling your heart muscle like a speed bag.

She placed a can and a frosted glass on the bar in front of me. "Cheers."

With the hockey game showing on the bar's TV screens, the conversation shifted to the Bruins' prospects for the upcoming season.

"They need more scoring if they want to contend this year," I said. "Aside from Pastrnak, who's gonna put the puck in the net consistently?"

"Everybody talks about scoring," Amalia countered, "but I think they need to be tougher on faceoffs and along the boards. They don't win enough one-on-one puck battles."

Amalia's family had come to the United States from El Salvador when she was fifteen. Although she hadn't grown up with frozen ponds or ice hockey, she quickly became a fan of the game's speed and physicality. As one of the few women to have completed the grueling Army Ranger School, she packed deadly force into her lithe, five-foot-four-inch frame. So it wasn't surprising that she would be drawn to a sport known for its violent collisions and gritty scraps for loose pucks in the corners of the ice.

Explaining the game's attraction to someone as cerebral as me was a little tougher. I suppose I liked the precision it required. Played at high speeds on blades only an eighth of an inch thick, hockey is a sport that requires quick mental calculations and crisp passes delivered to a moving target only a few inches wide—while players are traveling more than twenty miles per hour across a sheet of ice. When everything works in sync, the puck zipping along from tape to tape, it's exhilarating to watch. Such precise movement seemed to align with my own need for precision of thought.

"At least they have good goaltending," Kris said. "That should keep them in a lot of games."

Kris wasn't much of a sports fan by nature—she was much more comfortable watching a musical or curling up in front of a fire with a good romance novel—but she was learning to appreciate hockey for Amalia's sake and was a quick study.

The Bruins ended up losing the game, 2-1, on a late third-period goal. It was a continuation of a disturbing pattern that had begun the season before, where they weren't able to finish off their opponent at the end of games.

It reminded me of my own fortunes in the case involving the gun smuggling operation. Though I was sure Gordon himself was involved, I was unable to produce the evidence I needed to nail him for the crime. I'd had to settle for targeting him politically instead by campaigning on behalf of his opponent, gubernatorial candidate Lionel Hartman, in the election coming up that fall.

When the game was over, I finished my nonalcoholic beer, said goodbye to Kris and Mal, and left the bar.

Before achieving some minor celebrity in the gun smuggling

case, I had been driving a beat-up 1974 Dodge Dart that I'd bought at an auction. I loved that old car, but it stuck out like a neon sign in the middle of a sleepy, small-town center whenever I was doing surveillance work. That might have been okay when I was a small-time detective, but since the stakes had risen and I was taking on bigger (and more dangerous) cases, I'd grudgingly traded in my Dart for an unexceptional, metallic gray Honda Civic that blended in with the scenery much more effectively.

As I walked to my car along Merrimack Street, my mind was consumed by Bowles's unusual request. Despite what I'd said to Kris, I was intrigued by those peculiar entries in Cobb's journal.

Was there really a priceless treasure to be found inside a secret cache stowed away somewhere in southern New Hampshire? I was almost ashamed to admit it, but the thought had my pulse racing.

At the time, I had no way of knowing that I would soon receive yet *another* strange request inspired by a cryptic message that had been discovered by accident—and that this new case would make me forget all about the prospect of finding a hidden fortune.

Chapter 2

When I woke up the next morning, the sun was shining brightly and the temperature had already climbed to sixty degrees, suggesting that summer wasn't quite ready to retire.

I took Minerva, the four-year-old bloodhound I'd recently adopted, for a brisk trot along the Merrimack Riverwalk. When we got back to our apartment, I gave her a bowl of ice water and some leftover chicken breast. I also made a peanut butter and banana smoothie with chocolate protein powder for myself.

I had been listening to a lot of nineties music lately, and I opened a '90s playlist on my phone that began with "Supernova" by Liz Phair. As Ms. Phair sang about kisses "as wicked as an M16," I sat down in front of my laptop and set out to learn as much as I could about Walter Cobb.

From reading his obituary online, I learned that he was the youngest of three children. The Cobb family's money came from manufacturing toy trains and erector sets, and young Walter served in the U.S. Marine Corps before going on to college and becoming an architect. He worked for six years before retiring in 1988 at the still-green age of thirty-two so that he could travel the globe. As Bowles had indicated, he became a collector of fine art and antiquities from countries around the world.

If Cobb had been serious about acquiring a "priceless treasure" so sensitive in nature that he kept it hidden away and was unwilling to describe it in his journal, then I needed two critical pieces of information in order to find it: I had to know *what* I was searching for and *where* to look.

Using the databases I had access to as a private investigator, I ran a search to see if Cobb owned any properties aside from the family estate in Bedford, which he'd inherited in the late 1980s. My search yielded zero results; I couldn't find so much as a ten-by-ten storage unit rented in his name.

I also looked to see if Cobb was active on social media when he was alive. I was hoping I might learn something about the places he liked to go or locations that held a personal significance for him. But he didn't have a presence on Facebook or Pinterest or any other social media websites.

It looked like the only clue I had to go on was that journal entry dated August twenty-seventh, 1990. Three piddling sentences that didn't seem to carry much significance on their surface:

Stashed treasure from Romeo Hotel, Lima, with Beth/Meredith.
Key in C.
Corner lot, November 15.

Bowles had given me a photocopy of this journal page the night before, and I stared at the piece of paper intently, willing it to give up its secrets.

Aside from this photocopy, Bowles had also given me an itemized list of the artifacts he'd cataloged as part of Cobb's estate. There were European paintings from as early as the eighteenth century, as well as traditional African tribal masks,

Asian pottery, and musical instruments from cultures and societies spanning five continents, dating back to ancient times. These included a Mesopotamian lyre that was over four thousand years old, an Arabian lute, a collection of Chinese flutes, and drums and gongs from Indonesia.

Music was obviously important to Cobb. Could the phrase *"Key in C"* be a reference to a musical artifact? Or perhaps he'd devised a way to secure his treasure using a sound-activated locking mechanism, and the tune that unlocked it was intended to be played in the key of C major?

The phrase *"Stashed treasure from Romeo Hotel, Lima,"* suggested that Cobb had acquired his treasure either from, or while staying at, a hotel of that name. But an extensive Internet search revealed no such hotel in Lima, Peru—or Lima, Ohio, or any other U.S. state for that matter.

There was a Romeo Hotel in Naples, Italy, but I doubted it was the establishment Cobb had in mind. Maybe he was referring to a hotel that no longer existed? I could do some further digging on this point, but it would take more time.

"Corner lot, November 15." That could refer to almost anything. I did a quick search to see if anything significant happened on that date in 1990, and the only noteworthy event I found was the launch of the Space Shuttle Atlantis on a classified mission for the Department of Defense. Was it possible that Cobb was somehow connected to this classified shuttle mission?

Now you're just being spacey yourself, I thought.

Cobb's journal entry implied that he'd hidden the treasure with someone named Beth and/or Meredith. Again, I searched through all the databases I had access to for evidence of a connection between Cobb and anyone named either Beth or

Meredith. I also did a general Google search for *"Walter Cobb" and Beth or Meredith.* But all my searches came up empty.

I was hoping to talk with Cynthia Forrest at some point to see what she might know about her uncle's habits, and I made a mental note to ask her if she had any idea who these women might be.

I'd just spent three hours in front of my computer screen, and I'd made absolutely no progress on my treasure hunt to that point. Never mind Ben Gates, the character Nicholas Cage played in the *National Treasure* movies; I was more like Rusty Gates, old and firmly stuck in place.

Fortunately, I'd made plans to have a picnic lunch on Massabesic Lake with Callie Stewart, the woman I had been dating since July. Spending time with Callie was sure to improve my day dramatically.

* * *

I met Callie in the parking lot for Front Park on Route 28B in Manchester.

"Hey, you," she said playfully, greeting me with a smile that could stop the cars racing at the New Hampshire Motor Speedway in their tracks. She took my hands in hers and gave me a kiss that lingered for a few extra beats.

Callie was wearing a white vee-neck tee shirt, jeans, and sandals. Her long dark hair was tied back with a scarlet ribbon. As a dance instructor at a studio in Concord, she worked in the evenings, and we'd taken to meeting for lunch at least three times a week.

We walked along the lake shore toward the Massabesic Yacht Club and stopped at a spot right along the water. I took off the backpack I was carrying, pulled out a hand-sewn quilt that my grandmother had made, and spread it on the grass next to the lake. I also unpacked the picnic lunch I'd brought: sliced fruit with brie cheese and pesto chicken sandwiches with tomato and mozzarella on ciabatta bread.

"Catch any bad guys lately?" Callie asked me as she helped herself to some fruit and cheese.

I told her about my encounter with Bowles the night before.

"Oh, so I'm going out with Indiana Jones now?" she replied, her light gray eyes twinkling with mischief. "Where's your whip, professor?"

"I left it in the car with my bomber jacket and fedora."

The sky looked like blue topaz, and the sun felt warm on our faces as we ate our lunch by the lake. Despite the unseasonably warm weather, the leaves had already begun turning brilliant shades of red, gold, and orange.

The setting was so beautiful that I felt like I was in a painting.

"I know this is short notice," Callie said as she chewed on a slice of pear, "but my mom is having a barbecue lunch at her house this Sunday afternoon. It'll be mostly colleagues from UNH, including a fellow history professor she just started dating. But she's been eager to meet you, and she invited us to come along, too. If that's too much pressure, you can just tell me and I'll make up an excuse on your behalf—like you had to take Minerva to be dewormed or something."

I laughed. "No, that would be great. I'm looking forward to meeting her."

Callie's mother, Seraphina Durand, was a classics professor at the University of New Hampshire, and she lived in Durham. She was divorced from Callie's father, Rory Stewart, who was a lawyer. Seraphina was thirty years old when she had Callie, which meant she was sixty-seven now.

I knew that Callie's older brother, Jason, had died in a tragic skiing accident at the age of eleven, and her mother had suffered through crippling depression for months afterwards. I also knew Callie's mother had twin golden retrievers named Apollo and Artemis, and she was intrigued that my own dog was named after an ancient god as well, though I wasn't responsible for naming Minerva.

"What else should I know about your mother that you haven't told me yet?"

"Let's see… She was a competitive figure skater when she was a teenager. She has a soft spot for horses. Her favorite move is *Spartacus*. She chews on her lower lip when she's nervous. And, despite being a brilliant classics professor with more than fifty published papers to her credit, her guilty pleasures are reading Percy Jackson novels and watching Hallmark Christmas movies while eating peanut M&Ms."

"That's a lot to process. Think she'll like me?"

Callie looked me up and down with a critical eye, then titled her head back and forth, as if to say: "*Meh…*"

"She can be tough at first. But I'm sure she'll warm up to you. You have a way of growing on people."

"Yeah, like a fungus. Do you know anything about this guy *she's* seeing?"

"Only that his name is Ezra Liebowitz, he teaches seventeenth century European history, and he drives a black Porsche 930 Turbo—though my mom claims that has nothing to do with why she's interested in him."

"And how do you feel about the fact that she's dating someone?"

"Oh, I'm fine with it. It's not like I'm a child any more. And besides, this isn't the first guy she's been with since she and my dad were divorced. She's actually had several partners during that time."

"Do you two have the kind of relationship where you can talk about sex and stuff like that?"

"Yuck, no. We're pretty close—but not *that* close."

My cell phone rang, interrupting this idyllic scene by the water's edge. I gave Callie an apologetic look, then tapped the screen.

"Hello, Parker Hanson speaking."

The voice coming through my phone's speaker sounded anxious. "Mr. Hanson, my name is P.J. Warner. I'm hoping I can speak with you about an investigation."

"Thanks for calling, Mr. Warner. I'm in the middle of something right now. Are you available to chat tomorrow morning?"

"Well, um… The thing is, it's kind of an urgent matter. You wouldn't have time to talk this afternoon?"

"If it's urgent, why don't you try the police?"

"I *have* talked with the police. But they don't believe me."

"I'm sorry, Mr. Warner, but what's so urgent that it can't wait until tomorrow?"

Warner hesitated before responding, and what he said next made my stomach flip.

"I think someone might be planning a terrorist attack here in Concord next month."

Chapter 3

I met Warner at a secluded spot in West Terrill Park along the Merrimack River in Concord about an hour after he called. He was a young guy with a husky build who looked to be in his mid-twenties, with a shock of wavy dark hair falling across his forehead. He was wearing a gray tee shirt and black jeans, and five or six leather bracelets encircled his left wrist.

After we shook hands and introduced ourselves, Warner got right down to business.

"I'm an IT support specialist at the Best Buy here in Concord," he said. "A local church called the Kingdom of Light dropped off a laptop that was infected by a virus, and they asked us to fix it. As I was removing the virus, I noticed that one of the Word documents saved on the desktop had the file name 'Project Abaddon.' Are you familiar with that name?"

"No," I admitted.

"I play a lot of video games and fantasy role-playing games. The name 'Abaddon' comes up in these games quite a bit. Usually it's given to a real badass character, like a demon or an avenging spirit who's a high-level boss." Noticing the puzzled look on my face, he added: "A boss is a large or formidable character that players have to defeat at the end of a level if they want to advance in the game. Anyway, seeing a file with the name 'Abaddon' on the laptop piqued my interest, and so I opened the Word doc. And this is what I found."

He took a piece of paper from the back pocket of his jeans, unfolded it, and handed it to me.

It was a printout of what appeared to be a checklist:

- *Trig: hardware*
- *JK: building access*
- *RA: wheels*
- *Final prep Oct. 14*

Ezekiel 18: "The soul who sins shall die."

I wasn't sure exactly what I was looking at, but I understood Warner's gut response. The feeling I had when reading the quote at the bottom of the list reminded me of the first time I watched the original *Halloween* movie with Jamie Lee Curtis as a teenager.

"I googled 'Abaddon' to find out what it means in a Biblical context," Warner said. "Apparently, Abaddon is the name of the archangel who chains up Satan and casts him into the Abyss for a thousand years in the Book of Revelations, and he also tortures nonbelievers by unleashing a swarm of locusts on them during the End Times."

"Sounds like a real nice guy."

"Yeah. Given Abaddon's role as a punisher of sins, and the Bible quote at the bottom of the document, it looks to me like some members of the church might be planning a violent assault against a person or a group of people they consider to be unholy. And these bulleted items appear to be peoples' assignments in the plot."

For the second time that day, I stared at a piece of paper and tried to make sense of its ambiguous contents. As much as I looked for an alternate explanation, I had to admit that Warner's assessment seemed on the nose.

The words "final prep" suggested that Project Abaddon was a plan of some sort. And while I truly hoped this wasn't the case, the quote at the end seemed to imply that murder might be the plan's ultimate goal.

"JK" and "RA" looked like the initials of people involved in the plan. "Trig" could be the nickname of another co-conspirator. "Wheels" probably referred to a vehicle—maybe a getaway car?—and "RA" was either the car's driver or was tasked with procuring it. "Building access" suggested the group needed access to a certain structure in order to carry out the plan. *Was it intended to serve as a sniper's vantage point*, I wondered? If so, then perhaps "hardware" referred to the weapon the sniper would be using.

"That's what it looks like to me as well," I agreed. "You say you went to the police with this information?"

"I did. The sergeant I talked to said he would file a report, but there wasn't enough here to consider it a credible threat. I didn't get the sense that he was taking me seriously. Then I remembered reading about you and what you'd done in exposing that gun smuggling plot, and I thought maybe you could look into this threat as well."

"Who brought the laptop to you for servicing?"

"The guy's name is Brad Ackerman. He works in the church's administrative office."

"Is it his personal laptop, or is it a shared device that belongs to the church?"

"He said it belongs to the church. Basically, anyone who has access to its login credentials could have created that document."

"Do you still have the laptop?"

"No, Ackerman came back for it this morning. But I made a digital copy of the laptop's contents."

"Did you look on the device to see if there was any additional information that could have been connected to this plot?"

"I did, and I didn't see anything else that looked suspicious."

"Thanks, P.J.," I said, extending my hand. "You did the right thing in reporting what you found."

"So you'll look into it?"

"I will. And I have your contact information if I think of any more questions for you."

* * *

If Warner and I were interpreting the document titled "Project Abaddon" correctly, then a group of people affiliated with the Kingdom of Light Church might be planning an act of violence in a few weeks' time.

Of course, it was also possible that we were misreading the entire situation. But I couldn't just ignore the danger signs. Doing nothing might put the lives of who knew how many people at risk.

I had just agreed to help Peter Bowles confirm the existence of a hidden treasure the day before, and I wasn't about to back out on my promise to him. I was also committed to making sure New Hampshire Governor Jack Gordon wasn't reelected in the coming weeks.

Needless to say, I already had a lot on my plate. Accepting yet another case at this time would be like ordering berry-stuffed French toast on top of a Denny's Grand Slam.

On the other hand, the Bowles case wasn't time-sensitive, whereas Warner's information seemed pretty urgent. I felt like I should at least poke around to see if the threat might be real.

Normally, I would need an actual client before taking on an investigation like this. But in July, I had found the missing daughter of a man who'd fled from Honduras with his family and relocated in New Hampshire to escape political persecution in retaliation for protesting a corrupt government regime. He was so grateful that he'd offered me twenty-five thousand dollars in cash for my help. When I refused to accept his payment, he'd insisted, telling me to use the money to help those who couldn't afford my services themselves. I'd set up a charitable fund using the money he gave me, and I figured I could pay myself from this separate account as I looked into Warner's concerns.

Before driving back to Manchester, I stopped by the Concord Police Department to see my closest ally on the force, Detective Frank Connor. A tall Black man in his mid-fifties, Connor had been instrumental in helping me crack the gun smuggling case just a few months earlier.

As luck would have it, Connor was at his desk catching up on some paperwork when I asked the dispatcher if he was available.

"Hanson." He greeted me with a shake of his head, unwrapping a mini Tootsie Roll and popping it into his mouth as he did so. "To what do I owe the pleasure?"

"Got a minute to talk?" I asked.

He shrugged and led me to a vacant conference room.

"What do you know about the Kingdom of Light Church here in town?" I asked him as he closed the door behind us.

He looked at me askance, like I'd shown up at his house

wearing nothing but a silk robe and aviator glasses to pick up his daughter for a date. "Do I dare ask why?"

"Connected to a case I'm working. Ever had run-ins with any of their members? Or complaints about the organization itself?"

He looked uncomfortable, like he wanted nothing to do with this conversation. "Please tell me you're not investigating the church."

"I wish I could. What's the problem?"

"New chief's a member there. So are a few of the officers."

I'd worked with the former chief of the Concord PD, Colton Drummer, on the gun smuggling case, and I had a lot of respect for him. Drummer had retired in August, however, and I didn't know his replacement, Chief of Police Dalton Keane, at all.

"Well, that complicates things." I told him about my meeting with Warner, and I showed him the printout Warner had given me. "What do you think?"

"I can see why you and your friend might think it looks suspicious," he said, choosing his words carefully. "On the other hand, I can also see why that sergeant dismissed him. There's not nearly enough to go on here."

"Spoken like a true politician. Are you planning to run for office?"

"Parker, you know I'd like to help you. But while *you* might be able to operate on instinct, I don't have that luxury. *I* need hard evidence."

"Can you at least keep your ear to the ground?"

"Tell you what. You get me the identities of the people mentioned in this document, and I'll see what we have on them. And if you can bring me some actual proof of a crime being planned, then we'll open a full investigation. Right now, that's the best I can do."

* * *

When I got home from Concord, Minerva was curled up on the couch, napping. She woke up when she heard me sit down beside her, and she licked my face to say hello. I took her for a walk to Veteran's Memorial Park, where we played fetch with an old tennis ball.

Back at the apartment, I sauteed some julienned carrots, zucchini, and green beans in light olive oil while I cooked some couscous. I combined everything in a bowl, drizzled some balsamic vinegar on top, and sat down with my early dinner while I watched a classic episode of the '80s sitcom *Cheers*. It was the one where Haymitch from *The Hunger Games* is about to marry his rich fiancé, Kelly, but a comedy of errors unfolds on their wedding day—and Michael from *The Good Place* tries to keep the ceremony from spinning out of control.

My day ended the same way it began, sitting at my computer doing research. This time, I sought to learn as much as I could about the Kingdom of Light Church, or KL as it was referred to on its website.

From this site, I discovered that it was an evangelical Christian church with about eighty members. It was created in 2009 by a husband-and-wife team, Jonah and Olivia ("Livy") Keefe. Jonah Keefe ... *Was he the "JK" referred to in the Project Abaddon document?*

I looked throughout the church's website to see if there was a publicly available membership list or directory, something that would help me learn who the other people mentioned in the Project Abaddon document might be. But I couldn't find anything that helped me answer that question.

The language on the church's website seemed very welcoming and inclusive: *"We believe that everyone has value and is loved by God, and we're excited to have you join our community. We believe God has a plan and a purpose for all of us, and we look forward to helping you discover yours. Whoever you are and whatever path you might be walking, let's experience God's grace and love together."*

However, when I downloaded some of Jonah Keefe's recent sermons, the tone was quite different. They were fire-and-brimstone diatribes warning the congregation to atone for their sins or face the wrath of God's judgment.

Evangelical Christians interpret the Bible literally, believing it to be the unquestioned word of God. Yet, this message is filtered through many different prophets and apostles. To me, it's like when there are multiple writers credited in a screenplay: You know the resulting film is probably going to be pretty uneven. The producer or director wasn't happy with the script, and so they brought in other writers to fix the underlying problems—and the whole project ends up having too many different voices and no clear sense of cohesion.

God, the Holy Father, is a vengeful entity who tries to scare people into living a virtuous life by threatening eternal suffering for those who are immoral. Jesus, the Son of God, is a kind and benevolent deity who preaches love and acceptance of everyone. It's as if these Christian denominations are playing "good cop, bad cop" with their congregations' souls.

The Kingdom of Light Church clearly placed a lot of stock in the Bible's teachings of retribution and eternal damnation, seemingly more so than its messages of peace, love, and forgiveness. Was it possible that such violent messaging and imagery had inspired some members to dispense their own brand of justice to those they viewed as wicked?

After perusing the church's website, I expanded my search to the Internet at large. I wanted to see what others had written and said about the church online. Yet, aside from a few notices of church events in the calendar sections of local newspapers' websites, I found very little third-party information about the organization.

In searching for the phrase "KL Church," I was surprised to learn that KL was also an acronym for *Konzentrationslager*, the German word for "concentration camps." *Was this merely a coincidence*, I wondered? *Or, was it a deliberate choice in language that signaled something far more sinister?*

As nine o'clock rolled around, my vision began to blur from staring too long at a computer screen, and so I closed my laptop and went to bed. But I lay awake for a few more hours, gazing restlessly at the ceiling—my mind refusing to succumb to sleep.

There was a lot I needed to figure out about the nature of Project Abaddon. Was it a deadly plot as Warner and I suspected? Or was it something more benign? Was it even credible, or merely the warped musings of someone with no real intentions of carrying it out?

If it *was* a planned assault, who were the intended targets? Where and when would the attack take place? How would it be accomplished? Who were the participants referenced in the Word file that Warner had discovered? Who else knew about the plot or was involved in its execution?

Amid all these questions swirling around in my mind, a key phrase within the Project Abaddon document kept rising to the surface: "Final prep Oct. 14."

Today was Thursday, September thirtieth, exactly two weeks from that date. If the document that Warner had discovered was indeed to be taken seriously, then I didn't have a whole lot of time to learn the answers to those questions.

Chapter 4

Despite not falling asleep until after eleven p.m., I was up by four thirty the next morning. After taking Minerva for a brief walk around the block, I made myself a breakfast consisting of smoked salmon on toasted sourdough bread with nonfat cream cheese, accompanied by fresh blackberries. I took my breakfast in the car along with a flask of ice water and was parked down the street from the Keefe residence by five thirty.

Investigating a crime you think will take place in the future is very different from uncovering the details of an event that has already occurred. It's also much harder, because there's generally a lot less physical evidence you can look for.

How do you learn about something that hasn't happened yet?

Suppose you're in high school. You have a history test coming up during fourth period, and you're desperate to know what's on the exam. If your class is the first to take the test, then knowing what questions will be asked is no easy feat. You'd have to have seen your teacher creating the test, or overheard her talking about it with a colleague, or perhaps secured a copy of the exam illicitly.

But if another class has taken the same test during first

period that day, then suddenly the task becomes much easier. There are a few dozen witnesses you can ask. Maybe someone took a picture of the exam with their phone camera. Once an event has actually happened, a whole new course of investigative channels opens up.

This was the challenge I faced in trying to learn whether Project Abaddon was real, and if so, what it involved—and whether anyone's life was truly in danger.

If I had several weeks to work with, I could have infiltrated the Kingdom of Light Church, gained the conspirators' trust, and hoped they might eventually include me in their plans. But I didn't have the benefit of time. I needed information quickly, which was why I was staking out the Keefe residence at that ungodly hour of the morning (pardon the pun). I wanted to learn about Jonah's routine in particular, such as where he went and with whom he interacted throughout the day—with the hope that I might stumble onto some aspect of the presumed plot.

Jonah and Livy Keefe lived in a gambrel-style house with mocha-colored siding and white trim in the Concord Heights neighborhood of Concord. I had found their address in an online database while I was doing research on my computer the night before.

The first sign of activity in the Keefe household came just after six a.m., when I saw lights go on inside the house. But nothing else happened for a few hours.

To pass the time and keep my mind sharp, I ranked my favorite movies from each decade, starting with the 1940s and my all-time favorite film, *Casablanca*. For the fifties, I chose *Singing in the Rain*. The '60s were harder; after much deliberation, I settled on *Dr. Strangelove*, though *Psycho*,

Charade, and *The Sound of Music* were all strong contenders.

I found the 1970s to be even more difficult. *Star Wars. The Godfather. Chinatown. Jaws. The Sting.* How could I pick just one? I skipped ahead to the eighties (*Raiders of the Lost Ark*) and nineties (*The Sixth Sense*) before returning to the decade I was born and settling on *The Sting.* Though it might not have been the best movie made in that decade, it was the one that resonated with me most strongly. I had fond memories of watching it with my father as a child.

I was mulling over the 2000s and trying to decide between two Christopher Nolan films, *The Dark Knight* and *Memento*, when a brand-new white Chevy Tahoe backed out of the Keefes' garage with Jonah behind the wheel. I glanced at the clock on my dashboard, which read 8:43.

I waited until he'd traveled about a quarter of a mile down the road, then followed along at a safe distance.

Jonah led me to the Kingdom of Light Church on South Street in Concord without stopping, where he pulled into the church's lot and parked. He got out of his vehicle, unlocked a side door into the church, and disappeared inside the building, carrying a well-worn leather satchel.

I parked on a side street about a hundred yards away, where I had a good view of the church and its parking lot. From this vantage point, I settled in to watch and wait again.

Although the Kingdom of Light Church was a fairly new organization, historically speaking, the building itself dated back more than a century. During the course of my research, I'd learned that it used to be a Presbyterian church before that congregation folded and sold the building to the Keefes.

Built of red sandstone and brick, the church featured a front stepped gable above an arched stained glass window depicting a giant cross that radiated light. To the right of the gable, a single, towering spire stretched toward the heavens, its weathered copper roof tinged green with age.

Shortly before nine thirty, a blue Nissan Altima pulled into the church lot and parked. The driver's side door opened, and a young man with short dark hair emerged. He was wearing a collared, aquamarine-colored quarter-zip pullover and brown corduroy pants. He went into the church through the side door as well.

About fifteen minutes later, a black Ford F150 pickup truck pulled into the lot, and a big guy with floppy blond hair got out. He reminded me a little bit of Chris Farley. He was wearing a Scotch plaid flannel shirt, faded blue jeans, and hiking boots. He, too, went into the church through the side door.

I kept a pair of binoculars in my car, equipped with a cradle for attaching a cell phone in order to take magnified pictures. Using this device, I got close-up photos of both men, as well as their vehicles' license plates.

Nothing else happened for a couple of hours. Then, about ten minutes before noon, Jonah emerged from the church, still carrying his leather satchel. He got into the Tahoe and exited the parking lot.

I followed him again as he drove up South Street, turned right onto Route 202 and then left on Main Street, and parked in front of the curb a few blocks up the road.

I pulled into a space about half a block south of where Keefe had parked and watched as he got out of his car and headed inside the Barley House Restaurant, across the street from the New Hampshire State House building.

I waited five minutes, then got out of my car and traced his steps. As I passed by the restaurant's front picture window, I stole a glance inside.

Keefe was seated at a booth near the back of the restaurant, across from someone I couldn't see from the window. They looked like they were engaged in an intense discussion.

Unfortunately, the booths on either side of the one Keefe was sitting in were already occupied, or I could have slipped into one of them and tried to listen in on his conversation.

I entered the restaurant myself, sat down at the bar, and ordered a club soda with a lemon wedge. When my drink came, I paid the bartender immediately instead of running a tab.

I took a sip of my drink, then excused myself and headed for the bathroom, passing by Keefe's table on the way. Jonah was talking to his lunch companion in a low voice, and the only phrase I could make out as I walked by was "put your faith in God's hands."

Inside the bathroom, I washed my hands while I assessed how I looked in the mirror.

I was wearing a light cotton button-down shirt, blue jeans, and cross trainers. Average in every way, I had a remarkably forgettable face with fair hair and glasses … wait, what was I even talking about just now?

Anyway, it was a quality that served me well in my particular line of work.

On the way back to the bar from the bathroom, I had a good look at the person Keefe was sitting with. He was a gaunt man with a bushy black beard and hollow, sunken eyes. He was wearing a dark blue cable-knit sweater that was frayed in a few spots. I heard him say the words "I don't know if I can do it" as I passed by their booth.

I returned to my seat at the bar, downed my club soda in

just a few swallows, and then went back out to my car, where I waited for the two men to leave the restaurant. When the guy with the beard came out, I snapped his photo and also got a picture of his car—a maroon Chevy El Camino from the 1970s—along with the license plate.

Keefe came out as well and climbed into his Tahoe. I started my car and followed him again as he pulled out into traffic. He turned right onto Loudon Road, crossed the Merrimack River, and continued on for another few miles before turning right onto D'Amante Drive and pulling into the parking lot of a Home Depot.

I drove into the lot as well and nestled my car in between two oversize pickup trucks.

Was the man with the beard involved in Project Abaddon as well, I wondered? What did he think he couldn't do? And what was Keefe doing at this hardware and building supplies store? Was he picking up materials for the group's plot?

I decided to follow him inside to see what he might be purchasing.

Even early on a Friday afternoon, the Home Depot was bustling with activity. The shoppers seemed to be mostly contractors dressed in denim work clothes, picking up supplies for whatever their current job was during their lunch break—although there also looked to be quite a few homeowners shopping for items they would need for their home improvement projects over the weekend.

I grabbed a hand basket from a stack inside the entrance to make it look like I was just another shopper, and I trailed behind Keefe at a distance of some thirty feet as he breezed past the plumbing, electrical, and power tool aisles. He appeared to be heading for the paint section, where he stopped in front of the sample color swatches.

Keefe spent a few minutes comparing various shades of beige while I began to wonder what I was doing there watching him.

Unless Project Abaddon involved painting the houses of sinners a hideous shade of ecru, I felt like I was probably mistaken about his intentions in the store.

Or maybe it was an entirely different kind of project than Warner and I suspected—something more along the lines of interior design or construction?

Keefe put the swatches back in the color rack and disappeared down the aisle containing thinners and solvents.

Could solvents be used to make an explosive device, I wondered? Had the examination of color swatches merely been a ruse to throw off any suspicion by onlookers?

I casually strolled to the head of the aisle so I could see what he was doing. But when I looked down the aisle, he wasn't there.

As I stood there wondering where Keefe had gone, I was startled by a quiet yet commanding voice behind me.

"Would you care to tell me who you are—and why you seem to be following me?"

Chapter 5

I turned around to find the imposing figure of Jonah Keefe staring down at me.

He was thin and unusually tall, probably six foot three or four. He was dressed in a black turtleneck sweater and gray wool slacks. He wore wire-rimmed glasses that went out of style at least a decade earlier, and his short brown hair formed a distinctive widow's peak on his forehead. He looked like a more austere version of the young Steve Jobs, like the showman CEO of a local geological society.

So much for subterfuge. I'd gone and blown my cover on the very first day of surveillance.

Fortunately, the three years I spent on my high school debate team taught me how to think quickly on my feet. This skill had served me well several times before in my capacity as an investigator, and it did so again now.

"I, uh—I'm sorry, Reverend Keefe. I didn't mean to worry you. I was working up the nerve to approach you and introduce myself. My name is Parker Hanson."

I held out my hand, and Keefe shook it. For some reason, I expected his grip to be cold and weak, like a "dead fish" handshake. But I was surprised by how firm and strong it was, like he was trying to exert his dominance.

"I've been thinking of attending your services," I continued, "but I wasn't sure if it would be okay to just show up unannounced on Sunday. I've never been to a church before."

He looked at me skeptically for a few seconds. Then his face morphed into an expression of warm benevolence. "Yes, of course. Everyone is welcome in our church. How did you hear of us?"

I wondered if I should make up a lie. But I figured that if Chief Dalton Keane and other members of the Concord police force were members of the church, they might recognize me and reveal my true identity. So I decided to play it straight.

"From some colleagues in the Concord PD."

"Oh, really? Are you in law enforcement as well?"

"In a manner of speaking."

"What does that mean?"

"I'm actually a private investigator."

Keefe's expression changed again, but only for a fraction of a second this time. For a brief, fleeting moment, the look of suspicion returned. Then it was gone just as quickly, replaced by his friendly demeanor.

The change was subtle; to anyone who was not well versed in reading people, it might not have been noticeable. To a poker player, a beleaguered spouse whose partner has been cheating for months, or a trained investigator, it was clear he was suddenly wary.

"Well, Parker, I look forward to seeing you at this Sunday's service. Now if you'll excuse me, I have a few supplies I need to pick up for the church." And with that, he turned and walked away.

Since I could no longer follow Keefe without making my intentions clearly known, I saw no reason to hang around the

Home Depot any longer.

So I left.

* * *

Before driving home, I called a friend who worked for the Manchester branch of the state Division of Motor Vehicles. I gave him the license plate numbers of the two other vehicles I saw at the church that morning, aside from Keefe's Tahoe, as well as the plate number of the El Camino driven by the guy Keefe had lunch with at the Barley House Restaurant. He promised to send me the names and addresses of the vehicles' owners.

When I got back to my apartment, I checked my email. Near the top of my in-box, just below an offer for ten percent off my monthly cable bill if I reupped for two more years, there was a message from my DMV contact with the information he'd promised.

The owner of the Nissan Altima was Brad Ackerman, the young man who worked in the church's administrative office (and who brought the infected laptop to Warner's Best Buy store to be serviced). The F150's owner was a guy named Charlie Dawes, and he lived in Loudon. And the name of the thin, bearded fellow who drove the El Camino (and whom Keefe met with at the restaurant) was Trace Gladstone of Concord.

None of these men seemed likely to be the "RA" mentioned in the Project Abaddon document, unless the "R" stood for a nickname used by Brad. But any of them could have been the person referred to as "Trig" in that digital file—or they might have been connected to the plot in some other way.

Using the resources I had access to as a private detective, I could have learned if any of the three men had a criminal record—and if so, what their transgressions were. But the police had a much more robust database at their disposal that showed not just criminal convictions but also complaints, charges, and other valuable information.

Hoping to obtain this more complete picture on each of my persons of interest, I called Detective Connor to request background checks on all three.

"These men are suspects involved in your supposed church plot?" Connor asked me.

"They might be, yes."

"*Might* be?" he practically shouted. "You want me to run checks on some random guys who *might or might not* be connected to an enterprise that *might or might not* even be a crime?"

"Sounds like you're up to speed."

"Jesus, Joseph, and Mary," Connor responded. "I'll get back to you later."

* * *

Callie came over that evening after her dance classes ended. I made a late dinner for the two of us: salmon filets broiled with honey, soy sauce, and lemon juice, accompanied by sauteed asparagus and red bliss potatoes with chives.

Callie spent the night at my apartment, but she had to leave early the next morning to attend an all-day jazz workshop in Boston. I had promised Lionel Hartman's campaign staff that I would canvass for Hartman on Saturday, and I invited Amalia to come with me. I thought it would be more enjoyable to have some company for the day. But I also figured I might have better luck in knocking on people's doors with a female companion—especially if there were households where a woman was alone.

I felt a little guilty about setting aside the Project Abaddon case for a few hours, given that the "final prep" for this supposed plot was now just twelve days away. But I'd made a promise to Hartman and his campaign team, and it burned me up inside to think that Governor Gordon might serve yet another term in office after literally getting away with murder.

Plus, I was attending the Sunday service at the Kingdom of Light Church the next day, and I assumed my investigation would be much more productive at that time. I was more confident in my ability to discover the identities of the co-conspirators once I had access to the entire congregation.

As I was getting ready to canvass for Hartman, I got a call from Peter Bowles. He wanted to know how I was coming along on his treasure hunt.

Zoinks!

Since Warner's phone call on Thursday afternoon, I had completely forgotten about Bowles's investigation. It had taken a back seat to the more pressing case involving the Kingdom of Light Church.

"I'm working on a few leads," I told him, lying to buy myself some time. "I'll have more concrete information for you next week."

"So you think there's something to it after all?"

"I wouldn't say that yet. It's still too early to tell."

"Well, let me know as soon as you have something to report."

Before leaving my apartment, I called Walter Cobb's niece, Cynthia Forrest, and arranged to meet with her for lunch on Monday. I figured it was about time I focused some of my attention on Bowles's case as well.

Then, feeling like a rubber band that had been stretched to its limits, I headed downstairs to canvass, stopping by Amalia's apartment to get her along the way.

I had known Amalia for a few years now, and I was aware that she had two personas. There was the side she projected as a bartender and when hanging out with friends: cheerful and carefree, usually with an affable smile lighting up her face. And there was the fiercely driven side that she brought to any task or challenge standing in her way.

On this afternoon, she was wearing a honeydew-colored top, black jeans, and Doc Martens, and she carried the same look of intense resolve that had gotten her through Army Ranger School.

"Have you done this before?" she asked.

"Just once. I canvassed our apartment building and the surrounding neighborhood a few weeks back."

"Did you have any luck?"

"Honestly, I had a lot of doors shut in my face. Be prepared to be humbled today."

"Why bother, then? Does this even work?"

"According to research, face-to-face interaction with people through canvassing can increase voter turnout by five to ten percentage points—or at least that's what Hartman's campaign office says. Let me put it another way. About a third of the state's citizens favor Gordon, another third support Hartman, and the remaining third don't feel strongly either way or aren't engaged in the political process. It's our job to convince enough of that latter group to vote for Hartman. If even ten percent of Hartman's supporters can persuade just one undecided person to vote for him, that could spell the difference in the election."

* * *

Amalia and I canvassed the condominium complexes along

the east side of the Merrimack River in Manchester, knocking on roughly eighty doors in just under three hours.

About thirty of those knocks went unanswered, and another thirty people politely—or not-so-politely—told us to buzz off. But we also had about twenty substantive conversations with potential voters about Hartman's agenda and what voting for him in the governor's race would mean for the state.

Amalia proved to be a good closer. I wasn't surprised, as I'd seen what she was capable of when she set her mind to accomplish something. But she had a real knack for learning what issues resonated the most with voters, like health care, education, or job creation, and then concisely making the case for why Hartman was the best choice.

In between condo units, we chatted about the cases I was working on, among other topics.

"What's Kris up to today while you're here with me?" I asked her.

"She's on the steering committee for the LGBTQ+ History Month celebration that Concord is planning for later this month. She was supposed to be in a committee meeting all afternoon, so I was happy to help you canvass."

"You wouldn't rather have some alone time?"

"And do what, get my nails done?" she scoffed. "Besides, that prick Gordon and his *amigotes* tried to take you out multiple times this summer, and they shot at me for helping you. There's no way in hell I'm going to just stand by and let him get reelected—not without a fight, anyway."

* * *

Later that evening, I was back at my apartment, watching the Bruins battle the Buffalo Sabers in another meaningless preseason hockey game. The score was tied at two goals apiece during the second intermission when my phone rang.

It was Detective Connor, calling with an update on the profiles of those men I'd seen with Keefe the day before.

"Ackerman is clean, and Dawes has only one prior," Connor said. "A DUI from when he was twenty-two. But your pal Gladstone is another story."

"What do you mean?"

"Turns out he's an experienced killer—trained on the government's dime."

"You mean ex-military?"

"You got it. He's a former SEAL. Developed an addiction to alcohol after he left the service, and did an eight-year stretch up in Berlin for applying his highly lethal skills in a bar fight with a very unfortunate loudmouth." Berlin was where the New Hampshire state prison for men was located.

"Whoa."

"Yeah. The jury found him guilty of second-degree murder."

As I thanked Connor and ended the call, I thought about what I'd just learned.

Gladstone had the skills required for a deadly assault, and he'd already killed before.

Plus, it hadn't escaped my attention that—roughly speaking—the first two letters of his first name and the first letter of his last name formed the nickname "Trig."

Coincidence? Maybe ... or maybe not.

Either way, it seemed I had a new suspect in the Project Abaddon plot to keep tabs on.

Chapter 6

After taking Minerva for a long walk on Sunday morning, I showered, shaved, and put on a white polo shirt, black trousers, and a gray tweed sport coat. Then I drove to the Kingdom of Light Church in time for the ten o'clock service.

Aside from weddings and funerals, I hadn't attended an actual church service in more than thirty years.

It wasn't a great experience, which is why I hadn't been back.

When I was twelve, my parents—who weren't really churchgoers themselves—sent me to vacation Bible school to make sure I had some exposure to organized religion. But the religious education teacher grew tired of my questions after only the first day.

"The Bible says God is perfect," she told us in the morning, and later that afternoon, she noted: "In the Book of Exodus, God warns: 'You shall have no other gods before me.'"

"Why would God say that, if He really is perfect?" I interjected. "You told us that pride is a sin. But isn't telling His followers to worship only Him and no other gods an act of pride? Why should God care who people worship, if He isn't a jealous being? For that matter, why would He punish someone who doesn't believe in Him, even if they're a good person? Isn't that being both prideful *and* wrathful? And what about Jews and Muslims and Hindus? Do you really think they're all going to Hell, just because they happen to believe in the wrong god?"

"My, Parker, you're certainly full of questions," she responded with a taut smile. "But church isn't a place for questions. It's a place for faith and belief." And she forged ahead with the lesson.

That was all I needed to hear to know that church wasn't a place I cared to spend my time.

Asking questions, I believe, is what naturally curious people do. It's what led me to become a reporter, and then an investigator. To me, a world without questions is about as desirable as a world without light or oxygen.

Now that I'm older, I realize that not all churches discourage inquiry or critical thought—and some actually welcome these as a way to discover or affirm universal truths.

But that early memory had tainted the idea of organized religion for me. And based on the brief taste of the Kingdom of Light Church I got from the sermons posted to its website, I wasn't optimistic that it would encourage many questions, either.

Still, I resolved to keep an open mind as I approached the building's front doors that morning.

As I entered the vestibule, I was greeted by a woman wearing a peach-colored blouse and a black, knee-length skirt. She had shoulder-length blond hair and a pleasant smile. A name tag affixed to her blouse read *"Hello. My name is Pam."*

"Welcome to our church," she said, extending her hand. "I'm Pamela Arsenault, but everyone calls me Pam. I'm the chair of the hospitality committee."

"It's nice to meet you, Pam. I'm Parker Hanson."

"I haven't seen you here before. Is this your first time?"

"It is."

"Well, we're glad to have you here! Let me know if you have any questions."

"Actually, I do have a few questions I'd like to ask you. Can I find you after the service?"

"Sure. I'll be downstairs for coffee hour."

Inside the church, high vaulted ceilings soared above the heads of the parishioners, supported by thick stone columns. The scent of aged wood and paraffin candles filled the air. Rows of wooden pews stretched down the aisle toward the altar at the far end of the building, which was draped in rich fabric and adorned with gold accents. The entire church was illuminated by natural light streaming through the stained glass window at the front.

I took a program of service and settled into a pew in the back left corner of the church.

As I was glancing through the program, Concord Police Chief Dalton Keane sat down in the pew beside me. I introduced myself and said: "You like to be able to see the entire room at once, too, don't you? Same as me."

"Force of habit for a lawman, I guess."

Jonah and Livy Keefe sat in high-backed chairs on either side of the altar, and an organist played solemn hymns as the church continued to fill. Jonah wore a charcoal-colored suit and tie. Livy wore a purple flowered dress, and her raven-colored hair was done up neatly in a bun.

At ten o'clock sharp, the organist stopped playing, and a hush fell over the church.

Livy stood up in front of the altar. She made a few brief

announcements and led the congregation in prayer. Then Jonah took over and delivered his sermon:

God is all-encompassing love. In fact, God loves us all so much that He is waging a great battle on our behalf.

It's a battle of good versus evil. And folks, let me tell you: Although He is almighty, He is losing a little bit more of that battle every day—for the wicked are multiplying in number.

God is eternal light. But He has no tolerance for the darkness.

The kind of darkness that invades the minds of men who dress up as women. That infests the hearts of whores who seek carnal pleasures. That corrupts the souls of groomers who prey upon children.

Our society is run afoul with all manner of sinners. Those who are perverse in their beliefs and habits, wicked in their thoughts and deeds.

Drug dealers who lure others with the promise of a moment's ecstasy, only to deliver a lifetime of addiction and pain ... and addicts who are weak enough to succumb to that temptation in the first place.

Status seekers who are beholden to their jobs and their cell phones, instead of answering to the higher calling of God.

Thugs and thieves who have chosen a life of crime instead of service to society.

Welfare queens and idle beggars who are content to live off the labor of others instead of supporting their families.

Women who defy their husbands, and anyone who doesn't know their place.

For these people, Judgment Day is coming. But I have good news: God is also forgiving. He is willing to overlook the sins of men and women if they renounce the errors of their ways and accept Him into their lives...

Jonah was still talking, but I had tuned him out. I was thinking about how, if I was right about the nature of Project Abaddon, there was no shortage of potential victims the plot could target, based on the litany of "sinners" he'd just identified in his sermon.

Some, like drug dealers and career criminals, were worthy targets for scrutiny, if not for a physical attack. But *women who defy their husbands? Anyone who doesn't know their place?* That sounded like something straight out of the pages of *The Handmaid's Tale* or *To Kill a Mockingbird*.

And yet, there must have been at least fifty people listening attentively to the sermon. I shuddered to think that so many people in a relatively progressive part of the country could still embrace such nineteenth-century thinking.

* * *

When the service was over, the congregation headed downstairs for coffee and refreshments. Forgoing the coffee, I sought out Pam Arsenault, who introduced me to her husband, James.

"Really?" I said. "You're Pam and Jim? No kidding."

"It's James, actually," he replied, failing to understand my amusement.

Maybe he preferred the British version of *The Office*.

"How did you like the service?" Pam asked.

"It was … *illuminating*," I said, trying to be diplomatic.

"Oh good," Pam said, interpreting my adjective in a different way than I'd intended. "I'm glad you found it instructive. You said you had some questions for me?"

"Yes. Do you have a church directory or something that lists the names and addresses of members?"

"We do, but it's only available to members. Would you like

to join our community?"

"Sure. How do I do that?"

"You can sign our pledge book on the way out today. You'll get a copy of the directory and some other basic information in your email within a few days."

Pam and James introduced me to a number of other parishioners, but none of them had the initials "RA." I also briefly met Livy Keefe, who clasped my hands and gave me a cheerful smile. "We're grateful that you've chosen to attend our church," she trilled. "What is it you do for work?"

"I'm a private investigator."

"Oh, really? Like Magnum PI?"

"Yeah, I suppose—minus the red Ferrari and the mustache."

She looked puzzled. "What mustache?"

I had to be discrete about my investigation. I didn't want to tip off the co-conspirators that I was aware of Project Abaddon and was looking for more details, or else I risked being shut off completely from any access I might otherwise gain. I was limited, therefore, in what I could say to people without arousing their suspicions.

I figured I might have better luck in searching the building to see what information I could find, like maybe a written record of the plan. The fact that everyone was downstairs having coffee and refreshments gave me an ideal opportunity to snoop around.

Once I'd disentangled myself from the Arsenaults, I walked back upstairs and passed through the sanctuary. On one side of the nave, I found a door that led to a hallway. The side door I'd seen Jonah Keefe and the others use to enter the church on Friday morning opened into this hallway as well.

To my left, the hallway ended at the door to the church's

administrative office. I tried this door, and it was unlocked. I slipped inside and quickly rummaged through the desk drawers and the hanging folders inside them, looking for some clue as to what Project Abaddon was and where and when it would take place. But I saw nothing of interest.

I left the room and eased the door shut behind me. Down at the opposite end of the hallway, another door stood ajar. I approached that door and was about to push it open when suddenly it swung inward—and there, framed in the doorway, stood Jonah Keefe.

"We meet again," he said, sounding like a villain in a Bond film.

"Yeah," I countered.

Smooth, Parker. You've still got it.

"What are you doing up here?"

"Oh, uh … I'm looking for a bathroom. I seem to have gotten lost."

"The bathroom's downstairs," Jonah said. He came out into the hallway, shut the door, and locked it with a key—but not before I managed to see inside the room. It appeared to be his personal office space; I noticed a desk and a filing cabinet.

"Here, I'll walk you downstairs," he said. "What did you think of my sermon?"

"Awfully judgmental, wasn't it?"

Keefe smiled. "According to Second Corinthians: *For we must all appear before the judgment seat of Christ, so that each one may receive what is due for what he has done in the body, whether good or evil.*"

I didn't respond out loud. After all, what good would it do? There wasn't a chance that anything I said would change his opinion.

But in my mind, I thought: *What about, "Judge not, lest ye be judged?"*

* * *

As I left the church, I winced at the thought of what I'd just experienced.

Religion is supposed to lift you up. It's meant to make you feel good and inspire you to be a better person—or that's what I believe, at least. When delivered well, a sermon should fill you with awe at the grace and beauty of God's creation, not anger at people whose values or lifestyles are different from your own.

I felt slimy and gross, as if I'd just waded through dingy swamp water up to my chin. I wanted nothing more than to take a long, hot shower, to rinse away the residue of so much bile and hatred.

But there was no time for that. I was already late in picking up Callie. We were due at her mother's house in Durham in less than an hour.

Callie lived in an apartment in Concord that she used to share with her friend Maggie Malone. Maggie was a standout political reporter whom I'd worked with at the *Concord Herald* back when I was a journalist myself. She was killed when the car she was driving was deliberately rammed by a dump truck only four months earlier.

Callie had struggled through weeks of grief after Maggie's passing, but she was coping much better now. She had even found a new roommate, a dental hygienist named Hannah Bromfield who sang romantic ballads with a jazz-rock quartet called the Touch Tones at local restaurants three nights a week.

When I rang the doorbell to their apartment, Hannah answered the door. "Come on in," she said. "Callie's just drying her hair."

I sat down on the familiar blue barrel chair that I often used when visiting Callie's apartment and waited for her to be ready. When she emerged a few minutes later, looking ravishing in a slate-gray sheath dress and a camel-colored, button-down sweater—my favorite of the cardigans that hung in her closet—I told her about my experience at the church service and how unpleasant Keefe's sermon had made me feel.

As we were walking out to my car, Callie leaned on my shoulder. "Bravo to you for sitting through that service this morning without losing your mind," she said. "I don't think I could have done it."

A jolt of electricity coursed through my entire body, like I'd just stepped on a live wire—and I stopped abruptly.

"What did you say?"

"I said I was glad I didn't have to sit through that service like you did this morning."

"No, before that."

"You mean, *Bravo to you?*"

"Yes, that's it." The clouds inside my mind suddenly parted, and a bright ray of sunshine beamed down, casting the words that Walter Cobb had written in his journal in a whole new light.

As I realized I might have just made my first breakthrough in either of the two cases I was working on, a smile slowly spread across my face.

"Callie, I could kiss you!" I exclaimed.

"Well," she replied, looking up at me with a coquettish grin, "don't leave a girl hanging."

Chapter 7

As we were seated in my car, heading east on Route 4 toward Durham, I explained to Callie the epiphany I'd just had.

"Walter Cobb wrote in his journal: 'Stashed treasure from Romeo Hotel, comma, Lima, comma, with Beth-slash-Meredith.' I assumed from the way he used those commas that he was referring to a place called the Romeo Hotel, located in the city of Lima. I think that's what he wanted anyone who read his journal to assume. But now I believe Cobb stuck those commas in to throw potential readers off the trail."

I continued: "Romeo, Hotel, and Lima are all code words for letters in the NATO phonetic alphabet, which is used by radio operators in the military and other contexts to communicate more clearly and avoid confusion about the names of letters that sound alike. When you said 'Bravo,' which is the code word for the letter 'B,' it helped me make this connection. Cobb served in the Marines, which means he would have been familiar with the NATO alphabet himself."

"So you think Cobb was really writing that he stashed the treasure from *R-H-L* with Beth and Meredith?" Callie asked.

"Yes, that's what I think."

"Then what does R-H-L refer to?"

"That's what we need to figure out."

Callie searched on her phone for possible meanings of the acronym "RHL."

"There are lots of things those letters could stand for," she said, rattling off several examples. "Red Hat Linux, a version of the open-source Linux operating system that was discontinued in 2004. The Russian Hockey League. Richardson-Hill Limited, a health and safety consulting company based in London. The Rhodes House Library at Oxford University."

"The last one sounds interesting. What can you find out about that Oxford library?"

"Rhodes House was built in memory of Cecil Rhodes, an alumnus of the university and a major benefactor," Callie said, reading from the library's Wikipedia page. "Ahhhhh," she added, looking up from her phone, "he was the guy the Rhodes Scholarships are named after."

"Does the library have any collections that would be considered valuable?"

"Maybe, yeah. It says here that Rhodes House contains a significant collection of paintings, portraits, and busts, with subjects including Queen Elizabeth the Second, Nelson Mandela, and Rhodes himself. Maybe some of this art ended up in Cobb's hands?"

"It's a possibility."

I drove in silence for a few minutes as I thought about what Callie had just learned.

Of all the options she'd listed, the Rhodes House Library at Oxford seemed the most promising. Not only did it appear to be the most likely scenario, but it even housed a collection of what I presumed were valuable works of art, one of which might be the "treasure" Cobb was referring to. Yet, I couldn't just dismiss the other possibilities out of hand until I had thoroughly checked them out.

Maybe it was because I had hockey on the brain after watching the Bruins over the past week, but the Russian Hockey League also intrigued me. *What item of value might have derived from a foreign hockey league*, I wondered?

Russia was a major producer of many precious metals, such as copper, gold, and platinum, as well as oil and natural gas. Were those resources somehow connected to a professional hockey league? Or, maybe the treasure was a memento from an important player or game?

"We can eliminate Red Hat Linux from the conversation," Callie said, interrupting my train of thought. "I was just doing some more research online, and I found out it wasn't introduced until 1995."

"What if Cobb was somehow involved in the software's development, and he had some of the source code?"

"I can't see how that would be worth anything, if it's open-source."

"Oh, yeah. Good point."

Callie continued typing and swiping on her phone. "It looks like the Russian Hockey League isn't an option, either. It started as the Soviet League in 1946, and then became the International Hockey League in 1992 when the Soviet Union collapsed. It wasn't called the Russian Hockey League until 1996."

"So, the Rhodes House Library is looking more and more attractive," I said. "How would you like to take a trip to England with me?"

"Really?" Callie perked up. "Bloody hell! Sounds like a banging good time."

***

Callie's mother lived in an expansive Victorian-style home with a wraparound porch and a fenced-in backyard. An impeccably trimmed hydrangea bush bordered the red brick paving stones leading to the front steps of the porch, though its lavender-colored blossoms had begun to fade with the onset of fall.

"Parker, hello! It's so nice to finally meet you," Seraphina said as she greeted me at the door with a hug.

"Hi, Mom. I'm here, too," Callie deadpanned, giving her mother a peck on the cheek.

Seeing mother and daughter standing side by side was a surreal experience. Seraphina had the same long, lustrous hair and mischievous gray eyes as her daughter; the only difference was the streaks of gray marking the elder woman's tresses. She looked like an image of Callie that had been digitally altered to reflect the passage of time in a missing persons file.

Callie's mom ushered us into a cozy front parlor, where she introduced us to her other guests.

Ezra Liebowitz was a charming-looking man with silver hair and a healthy tan. He was wearing thick-rimmed glasses, a faded denim shirt, and jeans. He told us that he taught about the Scientific Revolution that took place in Europe during the sixteenth and seventeenth centuries, and how breakthrough developments in fields such as mathematics, physics, astronomy, and biology at that time had profound effects on how humans viewed the world.

In addition to Liebowitz, there were three other guests at the luncheon: Gillian Ross, whose area of expertise involved the history of women in America, and Skip and Fanny Draper, who'd met at UNH and married a few years before. Fanny taught East Asian history, and Skip was a professor in the school's psychology department.

After half an hour of small talk and grazing on appetizers that included coconut shrimp and stuffed mushroom caps, we proceeded to the screened-in porch at the back of the house, where we were served baked haddock and chicken cacciatore.

"So, Parker," Seraphina said, "Callie tells me you're a private detective. That must be so exciting!"

I smiled. That was the common assumption people made about my line of work, though it didn't always align with reality.

"It can be, sometimes. But it's not like what you see in the movies or on TV. Mostly it consists of a lot of Internet research and sitting around, waiting for something to happen on stakeouts."

"What are you working on now?" Ezra asked.

I hesitated. There was no need to alarm everyone by telling them I was trying to learn whether a group of fundamentalist Christians were plotting a terrorist attack on some unknown date just fifty miles from our current location, especially when I wasn't even sure for myself.

On the other hand, the matter I was investigating for Peter Bowles seemed kind of silly to bring up. Although, if I played up the odd nature of his request, I could probably get a few laughs out of the group.

"Believe it or not, I've been tasked with trying to find a hidden treasure," I said, rolling my eyes for comic effect.

I told them the entire back story, feeling a little sheepish as I did so.

"In fact," I concluded, "Callie helped me figure out just today that this so-called treasure we're looking for has something to do with the letters R-H-L, though we're still trying to figure out what."

Ezra dropped his fork in surprise, and the clatter reverberated throughout the screened-in porch.

Everyone at the table turned to look at him.

"I, uh … I think I may be able to help you there," he said in a halting voice, fidgeting with his napkin as he spoke. "My study of the Scientific Revolution crosses over into other aspects of seventeenth-century Europe, including Baroque art. You can see the influence of new scientific discoveries made possible by inventions like the telescope and the microscope in the shifting focus from mythical and religious themes to more realistic and humanistic ones within Baroque paintings and sculptures, for instance."

He paused to take a sip of his wine, then added: "Anyway, this is all a long-winded way of saying that I happen to know 'RHL' is how the Dutch painter Rembrandt van Rijn signed some of his early works."

My mouth went completely dry, and it took a few seconds for me to unstick my tongue enough to talk.

"You mean, *the* Rembrandt? Not, like, some lesser-known cousin?"

Ezra nodded. "RHL stood for Rembrant Harmenszoon Leidensis, or Rembrandt, son of Harmen, from Leiden—the town where he was born."

"So, this … this fortune I'm looking for," I stammered. "You're suggesting it might be an *original Rembrandt*?"

"It very well could be," he replied. "And it gets better."

He took off his glasses and used his napkin to polish them, leaving us all in suspense for another moment.

As he commanded our full attention, it occurred to me that

he must have been quite a powerful lecturer when he stood in front of his students at UNH.

"It turns out," he resumed, after putting his glasses back on, "that three famous works from Rembrandt have been missing since 1990—the same year your Walter Cobb is supposed to have acquired his treasure."

II

Where the Art Lies

Chapter 8

"Are you familiar with the Gardner Museum heist?" Ezra asked.

I was only eleven years old when thirteen priceless works of art were stolen from the Isabella Stewart Gardner Museum in Boston in the early morning hours of March eighteenth, 1990. Even so, I think almost everyone who was in New England at the time remembers that event. It dominated the news reports for days and captured the public's imagination in a way that's increasingly rare as the media landscape becomes more fractured.

"I know a little bit about it, yes."

"Among the items taken in that daring robbery were three of Rembrandt's works. One was an etching only slightly larger than a postage stamp, called *Portrait of the Artist as a Young Man*. The second was an oil painting of a well-dressed husband and wife, called *A Lady and Gentleman in Black*. But it's the third work that is considered most valuable."

He paused again for effect before continuing.

"*Christ in the Storm on the Sea of Galilee* is among the largest of Rembrandt's works, measuring over four feet wide and five feet tall. It's also his only seascape, and it depicts the Biblical event in which Jesus calmed the storm as described in chapter eight of the Gospel of Matthew. This oil-on-canvas painting is estimated to be worth as much as a hundred and forty million dollars."

I let out a low whistle.

"And these paintings were never recovered?" Skip Draper asked.

"No. None of the stolen works have been found, and the crime itself remains unsolved to this day."

* * *

After the excitement of learning that my investigation might be connected to a decades-old crime had abated, the luncheon plodded on.

As Ezra collected the guests' dirty dishes and Seraphina put out an assortment of desserts that included a red velvet cake and chocolate-covered strawberries, Fanny Draper launched into a story about a student in her East Asian history class whose grandmother bought a Yuan-era Chinese vase at a flea market that ended up being valued at more than a quarter of a million dollars. That led to a discussion of the best finds on the PBS television series *Antiques Roadshow*—and whether any of the guests on that show were planted by the producers.

"It's killing you to have to make small talk, isn't it, when all you can think about now is getting on your computer and learning more about the Gardner museum heist."

Callie had noticed that I'd grown quiet, my mind preoccupied as it chewed on the startling new information it had acquired.

"Am I that predictable?"

"Don't worry. Your salvation is near." As soon as dessert was over, she fashioned an excuse for us to leave, and we said our goodbyes.

62

On the drive home, we discussed the gathering and assessed Callie's mother's new boyfriend.

"He seems good for her," Callie said. "And she seems happy."

"Yeah. He seems like a good guy, though maybe a little theatrical. When it comes to dramatic pauses," I said, halting for a few seconds in an imitation of Liebowitz, "there's no one better than Ezra."

Callie rolled her eyes. "How long have you been sitting on that one?"

When we got back to my apartment, Callie curled up with Minerva on the sofa and immersed herself in my copy of the Sunday *New York Times*, while I opened my laptop and dug into the largest unsolved art theft in history.

The first thing I did was log on to the website for the Isabella Stewart Gardner Museum to learn more about the stolen Rembrandts.

Portrait of the Artist as a Young Man (1633) is an etching less than two inches by two inches in size. It features Rembrandt from the neck up, his long, curly hair flowing from beneath what looked like a newsboy-style cap, his round face sporting a mustache.

A Lady and Gentleman in Black was also completed in 1633. The gentleman is standing near the center of the painting, staring straight at the viewer. He's wearing a wide-brimmed hat, and his face has a ruddy complexion. The lady is sitting in the bottom right corner of the portrait, looking off to the viewer's left. Her left hand is gloved, but her right hand appears bare. The entire right side of the canvas is in shadow. This oil painting measures fifty-two inches in height and forty-three inches wide.

The year 1633 must have been an especially productive one

for Rembrandt, because *Christ in the Storm on the Sea of Galilee* was painted then as well. It's a good example of *chiaroscuro*, or the use of bold contrasts between light and dark to add a highly dramatic element to a painting.

The canvas features a small ship with a single mast that's tilting steeply to the right as the rough sea tosses it about. Jesus is asleep in the boat's stern, and some of his disciples are trying to wake him, while others tend to the ship's deteriorating sails—and one looks like he's vomiting over the side. The left side of the work is brightly lit, and the right half is in shadow. According to the Biblical story the work depicts, when Jesus is awakened by the disciples' cries for help, he reproaches them: "Why are ye fearful, O ye of little faith?" and then rises to calm the fury of the storm.

After studying the missing Rembrandts, I broadened my search to learn more about the theft itself.

According to my research, there were two security guards working at the Gardner Museum on the night of the heist: Rick Abath, age twenty-three, and Randy Hestand, age twenty-five. At 1:24 a.m., Abath admitted two men dressed as police officers through a side door to the museum. The thieves claimed they were investigating a disturbance, but once they gained entrance to the building, they handcuffed Abath and Hestand and left them in the basement.

The thieves then proceeded to loot the museum over the next eighty-one minutes. In addition to the three works by Rembrandt, they took *The Concert*, one of only twenty-four known paintings by Johannes Vermeer and considered the most valuable unrecovered painting in the world, at $250 million. Other stolen works included five sketches by Edgar Degas and *Chez Tortoni* by Edouard Manet. Altogether, the stolen artwork is valued at more than $500 million.

The thieves' movements were recorded by infrared motion detectors. Interestingly, this information revealed that the thieves never set foot in the museum's Blue Room, where Manet's *Chez Tortoni* was located. This led the police to speculate that Abath had taken that painting off the wall himself as he was making his rounds earlier in the evening.

Abath also opened and closed the side door earlier that night, and police suspected he might have been signaling the thieves. Abath, who died in 2024, maintained he had nothing to do with the heist and was never charged.

The FBI took control of the investigation, claiming the stolen artwork was likely transported over state lines. Although there have been many theories about the case, agents believe the robbery was planned by someone with ties to organized crime in Boston and that the two men who committed the crime are now deceased.

Despite countless hours of interviews and testimony, the location of the stolen works remained a mystery.

Nothing I read about the case suggested that a private art collector in New Hampshire might have one of the stolen paintings. But if Ezra Liebowitz was correct in his assessment, then I might be on the trail to discovering an item that had eluded highly skilled FBI agents for years.

Who knows—I might even become a key figure in solving a crime that had baffled the some of the greatest minds in law enforcement for decades!

I closed my laptop and set it aside. Picking up a throw pillow from the sofa, I bonked Callie lightly on the head with it.

"Oh, good, it's play time." Callie stood up and stretched her arms. Then she leaned down and gave me a long, slow kiss that served as a preview of coming attractions. "I'm just going to take a shower first."

As she headed for the bathroom, she called back over her shoulder: "Can you imagine if you're able to find a missing Rembrandt? We'd be the toast of the entire art world."

"Sure," I said, picturing the scenario in my mind. "But don't buy your Met Gala dress just yet. I have no idea where to start looking."

<h1 style="text-align:center">Chapter 9</h1>

As a private investigator, one of the parts of the job I hated the most was updating clients on the status of their cases.

Often, this meant delivering bad news—like their spouse was cheating or their teenage daughter was responsible for stealing their prized bracelet. Sometimes, the bad news was simply that I had nothing to report yet, or—despite my best efforts—I wasn't able to make any headway on their request.

But occasionally I did have some good news to pass on. Like when I united a local woman named Estelle Matthews with her son, Ray Johnson, whom she'd given up for adoption when she was just sixteen. Or when I located the missing daughter of Honduran refugee Emmanuel Machado just this past July. (It turned out she'd been kidnapped off the street and unlawfully detained in a federal ICE facility in Dover for two weeks, unbeknownst to her parents—and we had to work with a team of lawyers to have her released.)

Those joyful family reunions were among my favorite moments with clients. But the conversation I had with Peter Bowles on Monday morning was also one of the better ones I've experienced.

Bowles ran his estate sale company out of his home in

Nashua. I met him there at nine thirty to tell him what I'd learned the day before.

Upon hearing that, not only was I convinced Cobb's journal entry was real, but there was a good chance it was linked to a missing masterpiece from the Baroque period—not to mention a decades-old crime that had taken the art world by storm—Bowles nearly choked on the lime-flavored Perrier he'd been sipping.

"You're telling me we're looking for a stolen *Rembrandt*?" he asked incredulously.

"I believe so." As with Callie, however, I cautioned him that I was still far from knowing its actual location.

Bowles seemed positively giddy as he skipped out of the room and went to retrieve Cobb's journal. "Here, take this," he said, handing me the book. "Maybe there's something else in here that can help you find it. And if you need anything else from me, just let me know."

* * *

I was scheduled to meet with Cynthia Forrest for lunch at the Brickhouse Restaurant in Milford at noon.

Rather than drive home first, I headed directly to Milford, parked along Union Square, and sat on a bench in the gazebo within the Milford Oval—the town common that was actually more of a triangular shape—to read through Cobb's entire journal.

It made for pretty dry reading. I'd waded through software user agreements that were more exciting. As the designated time for my lunch with Ms. Forrest approached, I was grateful for the interruption.

Cynthia was a well-dressed woman who appeared to be in her mid to late forties. She wore an expensive-looking gray silk blouse and black pants. Although she had a certain elegance about her, I didn't get the sense that she was stuffy or put on airs; she seemed pretty down to earth.

"I'm sorry for your loss," I said as I introduced myself.

"Thank you. Mr. Bowles seems to think my uncle had some kind of hidden treasure? I don't know how useful I'll be in helping you find it, but I'm happy to try."

We sat at a table near the restaurant's floor-to-ceiling front window, with a view of the gazebo on the Oval. I ordered a Mediterranean salad topped with grilled scallops, and Cynthia asked for a cauliflower-crust pizza with artichoke hearts and sun-dried tomatoes.

When our waitress left the table, I started in with my questions.

"How well did you know your Uncle Walter?"

"I called him Uncle Walt. He was my dad's brother. I saw him a lot when I was a little girl. He didn't have any children of his own, and I think he looked at me as the daughter he never had. But then as I got older, he was traveling a lot—and I didn't see him as much."

As Cynthia was talking, I noticed that her features seemed to sag.

"You look sad all of a sudden. How come?"

She looked down at her plate for a few seconds, then back up at me. "When I said that Uncle Walt didn't have any children of his own, that wasn't completely true. I remembered that he did actually have a child with a woman he met while on leave in the Marines. But that child was stillborn. He never really talked about it, but I could tell the memory pained him. There was a kind of sadness about him. I don't think he ever got over it."

"I'm sorry to hear that. You said he traveled a lot. Did he have any favorite places?"

"He loved Cape Cod. He vacationed a lot on the Cape. He also talked a lot about San Francisco and the French Riviera."

"Did he own any properties in those locations? Any particular haunts within those regions that held a special meaning for him?"

"Not that I know of. He liked to stay at the Ocean Edge Resort in Brewster when he visited the Cape. But I don't know much about those other places."

"Did you know anyone named Beth or Meredith who might have been connected with your uncle?"

She thought for a minute. "There was an Elizabeth that Uncle Walt worked with at the architecture firm. He mentioned her a few times. I don't know her last name, but the firm could probably tell you."

* * *

Cynthia didn't know anything else that could help with the case, but at least she was a pleasant lunch companion. After we said our goodbyes, I returned to my car and followed up on the most promising lead I'd gotten from her.

Walter Cobb had worked for an architectural firm in Boston called Seaport Design for six years before retiring to lead a life of travel and leisure. I called the firm's main line and was connected to a receptionist. I introduced myself and noted that I was a private investigator trying to track down a long-lost piece of artwork.

"You had an employee named Elizabeth something—I'm sorry I don't know her last name—who worked for your firm during the nineteen eighties, and she might have some information that could help me in my search. I'm hoping you can help me get in touch with her."

"Gosh, that was so long along," the receptionist said. "Well before my time here. Let me take down your number, and I'll ask around and have someone get back to you."

* * *

In my conversation with Cynthia, she'd mentioned Brewster, Massachusetts, as a place where her uncle liked to go. I didn't have any plans for the rest of the day, so I figured I would drive down to Brewster to see if I could find a connection between the town and Walter Cobb that might lead to the painting's location. If nothing else, it gave me an excuse to visit Cape Cod for the afternoon.

By three o'clock I was driving over the Bourne Bridge onto the Cape, and by three thirty-five I was on Route 6A in Brewster.

Knowing that Cobb liked to collect fine antiquities, I stopped at every antique shop I came across in town and asked the owners if they knew him. But none did, at least by name. I also had the same response at The Brewster Store, the old-fashioned general store that had served as the town's social and geographical hub since the 1800s.

I visited the Brewster Town Hall and asked if they had any record of a Walter Cobb paying property or excise taxes there. That, too, proved to be a dead end.

Undaunted, I continued on to the Ocean Edge Resort. I parked in front of the sprawling mansion that served as the resort's main building and went inside, where I asked for the manager.

A distinguished-looking gentleman with neatly trimmed gray hair appeared and introduced himself as Carl. He was wearing a blue pin-stripe suit, and his shirt looked freshly starched.

"You've had a frequent guest here by the name of Walter Cobb," I said. "Do you happen to know him?"

Carl looked like the type of manager who would know his regular guests by name, and I wasn't disappointed. "Yes, sir, I know Mr. Cobb."

"When he stayed here, what did he like to do? Did he have any favorite places he liked to visit? Any regular restaurants, habits, activities—things like that?"

"I'm sorry, sir, but I can't talk about another guest like you're asking. Our clients appreciate their privacy. I'm sure you can respect that."

"Oh, it's okay," I replied. "Mr. Cobb won't mind. I'm sorry to say that he passed away a few weeks ago. I've been hired by the manager of his estate to find something of value he might have hidden away." I gave Carl my business card.

Carl looked at my card for a moment, then used it to scratch his chin while he thought.

"He liked to try new experiences. He was always asking for the staff's recommendations for places to eat and things to do. If he had any favorites, I didn't know about them."

"What was Mr. Cobb like?"

"Very friendly. Always polite to the staff. But also quite serious. I can't say I ever saw him laugh."

"Did you ever hear him talk about someone named Beth or Meredith?"

"No, sir."

"Does the letter 'C' mean anything to you? Could it refer to something here at the resort, like a particular unit?"

Carl had been very patient with me to that point, but I think he was starting to become tired of my questions.

"Well, 'C' is for cookie, as I learned on *Sesame Street*. As for any connection to the resort, I don't have the slightest idea what it might mean."

* * *

I had pressed my luck too far, and I wasn't learning anything useful at the Ocean Edge Resort, anyway—so I thanked Carl and left.

The sky to the west was ablaze with orange and pink hues as I walked back to my car, and I felt my stomach rumble. Before heading back to New Hampshire, I stopped for dinner and dessert.

I hadn't found what I was looking for on the Cape. But the drive down wasn't a total waste of time.

I'd had a lobster roll at Cobie's. A hot fudge sundae at The Sundae School. And, because it was a Monday evening in early October, I could look forward to very little traffic heading home over the Sagamore Bridge.

Chapter 10

I'd put in some time on Bowles's case, and now I was back to focusing on Project Abaddon and whether it posed a real threat.

From what Detective Connor had mentioned the other day about Trace Gladstone's violent past, I had come to suspect that he might be part of the plot—and that maybe he was the individual referred to as "Trig" in the document that Warner had found.

When I got home from the Cape on Monday night, I was still wired from the long drive. Instead of going right to bed, I'd stayed up doing some Internet research on Gladstone.

I learned that he was thirty-eight years old. He grew up in Hooksett, graduated from Manchester High School West, enlisted in the Navy at age eighteen, and married his high school sweetheart, Katrina McAdoo, a year later. They had a daughter together, Tricia, who was now eighteen and studying cosmetology.

Gladstone was in the Navy for eight years, serving on an elite Sea, Air, and Land Team. When he left the service, he worked at a manufacturing plant in Concord. But he also began drinking heavily. Katrina divorced him and moved back to Hooksett with Tricia, and one year later, he got into the bar fight that landed him in prison. He'd been out of jail for about a year, but I couldn't find any information about what he was doing at present and whether he had a job.

Now, at five o'clock on Tuesday morning, I was parked down the street from the mobile home in Concord where Gladstone lived alone.

It was trash day, and I had put on a pair of nitrile gloves from the box I kept in my car for just such occasions. I had taken the two thirteen-gallon trash bags from the barrel in Gladstone's driveway and brought them back to my car, where I was currently picking through their contents to see if I could find any evidence of a planned assault.

Don't let anyone convince you that being a detective is a glamorous job.

To make the task slightly more pleasant, I was listening to the '90s playlist I'd started the previous week. With Harvey Danger's angst-ridden gem "Flagpole Sitta" playing in the background, I sifted through the garbage from the first bag: banana peels and coffee grounds; empty Marlboro packs; crushed Miller High Life cans and Doritos Cool Ranch bags; the remnants from numerous TV dinners.

Finding nothing useful, I moved on to the second bag's contents.

As Alanis Morissette, the OG of the angry breakup song, unleashed four minutes of searing emotion at being dumped in "You Oughta Know," and I listened in awe at how she managed to express both ferocity and vulnerability at the same time, I came across an envelope in the second bag of trash. It was addressed to Gladstone, with a return address in Hooksett.

Inside the envelope was a note written and signed by his ex-wife:

Dear Trace,

    I got your letter, and I'm worried about you. Please don't do what your thinking about. If not for yourself than at least for Trish. Think of your daughter and what that would do to her. Call me if you want to talk.

    —Kat

I had two thoughts after reading the note.

First, I was pleasantly surprised to see that anyone still sent handwritten correspondence. If the note had been texted, I never would have seen it.

And second, I wondered what action Katrina didn't want him to go through with. Did it have anything to do with a deadly assault? Was it possible that Trace had confided in her about the group's plans?

I would need to talk with Katrina at some point to see what she might know. But in the meantime, I was going to stick close to Gladstone to see what I could learn from watching him all day.

* * *

I spent the entire morning watching Gladstone's home, but I didn't see any sign of him.

I had done the day's Wordle (ARSON, guessed in four tries). I'd also done the *New York Times* Spelling Bee and Connections puzzles. Although I'd solved Connections on my last available try, I wasn't happy about one of the categories. How in the world were players who weren't fans of antihero TV shows expected to know that HOUSE, CASTLE, POPE, and WHITE belonged in the same category together?

I was thinking of how else I could occupy my time when my phone rang.

"Hello, is this Parker Hanson? My name is Elizabeth Zaccario, and I used to work for Seaport Design many years ago. I was told you've been trying to reach me?"

"Yes, Elizabeth. Thanks for calling me back," I said, mentally shifting gears to my other case. "When you worked for the firm back in the eighties, did you know a man named Walter Cobb?"

"Oh, yes. Walter. I haven't thought about him in ages."

"What was the nature of your relationship?"

"We were colleagues. We worked on a few projects together, and we also dated briefly. But he wasn't really my type."

"Oh, yeah? How so?"

"He was the sort of guy who folds his pants and hangs up his shirt before jumping in the sack with you. And when you're done making love, he wants to change the sheets instead of just lying there together."

"I get the picture, thanks. When was the last time you saw him?"

"Mmmm, I think it was on his last day of work before he left the firm."

"And you didn't keep in touch afterwards?"

"No, not that I can remember."

"One more question: Do you ever go by the name Beth instead of Elizabeth?"

"No. I prefer Liz, actually."

"Okay, Liz. Thanks for your help."

* * *

Ms. Zaccario didn't seem to be the Beth that Walter Cobb had referred to in his journal. And Gladstone still hadn't emerged from his burrow. It was starting to look like this day would be a bust.

I was debating how much longer I should remain on the stakeout when the door to Gladstone's mobile home opened. He came outside, got into his El Camino, backed out of his driveway, and sped off down the road.

I followed him to a small shopping plaza about a mile from his home. He turned into the plaza, parked his car, and got out carrying a navy blue duffel bag. I pulled into the plaza as well and watched as he entered a pawn shop, where he spent several minutes inside.

When he came out of the pawn shop, the duffel bag was empty. He stashed the bag in his car and then entered a liquor store just a few doors down from the pawn shop, where he emerged a few minutes later with a brown paper bag. He got back into his car and drove off.

As I continued following him, I wondered how many other people made that same sequence of moves in the course of a day. It seemed a little dangerous to have a pawn shop and a liquor store located so close to each other—but mutually beneficial for both businesses, I assumed.

Gladstone returned to his mobile home and went back inside with his purchase. It didn't take a lot of investigative skill to know how he'd be spending his afternoon.

I was curious about what Gladstone had sold in the pawn shop. And there didn't seem to be much point in watching his house while he was inside drinking all afternoon. So I returned to the plaza to talk with the pawn shop owner.

The guy behind the shop's counter was of medium height and above-average girth. He wore a black Alice in Chains concert tee shirt, and an orange baseball cap with the logo for the trucking company Schneider National covered his balding head. A multicolored phoenix tattoo adorned his right forearm.

He introduced himself as Bubba. I'd never met anyone named Bubba before.

"You a cop?" he said when I stated my request.

"Private investigator, actually."

Bubba scratched his nose. "You want that information, it'll cost you."

I suppose I should have appreciated his entrepreneurial spirit. After all, he was just trying to support his family. Mrs. Bubba and Bubba Junior had to eat.

But I was in no mood. I hadn't made any breakthroughs in the Project Abaddon case yet, and the last thing I needed was someone jerking me around.

Besides, I hated bullies.

Some people thought they could steamroll you if you weren't physically imposing. I'd spent much of my life trying to avoid confrontations with the Bubbas of the world. There was a time when I would have backed down to Bubba as well, played his game by reaching for my wallet and offering up a twenty.

But a few months earlier, I'd survived not just one but *four* attempts on my life as I tried to bring Governor Gordon and his cronies to justice. I guess that experience had lowered my tolerance for bullshit.

"How about a counter offer? You answer a few questions because it would help me out and it's the right thing to do. In return, I decide not to look too closely into *your* business."

"Whaddaya mean?"

"Think about it, Bubba. I investigate crimes for a living. You don't want to make an enemy out of me. How long do you think it's gonna take me to find whatever dirt *you're* hiding?"

Bubba took off his cap and scratched the top of his head with its bill. "Okay. I see your point. What'd you want to know?"

"The guy who came in about twenty minutes ago carrying a blue duffel bag. What did he sell you?"

"He had an autographed Tom Brady jersey from back in his Patriots days. His high school class ring. A hunting knife. Two handguns. And some country music CDs."

"How much did you give him?"

"Two thousand, cash. The jersey alone is probably worth that at auction."

"Did he say anything to you about why he was pawning this stuff?"

"Yeah. Said he might not be around for much longer. He wanted to do something right by his daughter, leave her some money when he was gone."

"Got it. Thank you."

"Hey, how 'bout at least buying something while you're here?"

"You got anything signed by Patrice Bergeron?"

"No."

"Maybe next time."

* * *

I thought about returning to Gladstone's home and continuing my stakeout. But I figured if he was drinking, he probably wasn't planning to go out again that evening. So I headed home instead.

On the way, I mulled over what I'd learned so far.

Gladstone was planning to do something that concerned his ex-wife. From what I'd overheard him say to Jonah Keefe, it appeared to be something he wasn't sure he could follow through with, suggesting he was having second thoughts. And based on what Bubba had just told me, Gladstone didn't intend to stick around the city much longer.

If Project Abaddon was a deadly assault as I'd assumed, then all the pieces seemed to be forming a picture in which Gladstone was at the center of the plot. Perhaps he was having a crisis of conscience. Then Jonah had convinced him to go through with the attack after all. Now, it looked like he was tying up loose ends before splitting town once the job was done. Or in case he was caught and sent to prison... or maybe even killed.

I was disappointed that the lead on Elizabeth didn't pan out in the search for the missing Rembrandt. On the other hand, Gladstone was emerging as a prime suspect in my other case.

There was a lot I still needed to learn about the nature of the Project Abaddon plot. For instance, I didn't know how, where, or when the attack would take place—or even if it was real.

But if it *was* real, it seemed increasingly likely that Trace Gladstone played a key role in the plan.

Chapter 11

Wednesday, October sixth, began with a bone-piercing chill that served as a stark reminder autumn was under way. The Bruins would be playing their first game of the regular season later that evening, and I woke up excited about the start of a new hockey season.

I wanted nothing more than to keep the momentum going on the Project Abaddon case by following Trace Gladstone again. But I'd made plans for a road trip to Boston to learn more about the disappearance of the three Rembrandts from the Gardner Museum. If I could figure out how one of those works ended up in Cobb's possession, I was hoping this might help me discover its current location.

After walking Minerva and gulping down a bowl of nonfat vanilla Greek yogurt with blueberries and drizzled honey, I was on Route 93 headed south toward Boston. "Seether," an ode to female rage from the '90s alternative band Veruca Salt, reverberated through my car's poor-quality speakers.

My first stop was the FBI field office on Maple Street in Chelsea, across the Mystic River from Boston. I was scheduled to speak with Special Agent Davis Reed, the guy in charge of art crimes for the bureau, at ten o'clock.

The FBI building rises eight stories about a fenced-in

parking lot, resembling a concrete cinder block with windows. I checked in at the reception desk, where I was given a visitor's badge and escorted to a conference room on the fourth floor.

At five minutes past ten, Reed strode into the room. He wasn't any bigger than me, maybe five-foot-nine and a hundred seventy-five pounds, but he had a lean-and-mean look to him. I was guessing he was all muscle beneath the steel-gray suit he was wearing. His tanned face was creased with frown lines, and flecks of silver dotted his coffee-colored, crew-cut hair.

After introducing himself, Reed uttered: "You said on the phone you might have a lead on the whereabouts of one of the stolen works from the Gardner Museum?"

"I think I know who possessed one of the paintings most recently, yes. But I don't know where it is. I was hoping you might have some information that could help me find it."

"*Possessed*, as in past tense?"

"That's right. An art collector in New Hampshire named Walter Cobb. But he died last month. Does that name ring any bells?"

"No, I don't know anything about a Walter Cobb."

"That's too bad. What can you tell me about your investigation that I can't find on Google?"

Reed glared at me for a few seconds. "Look, *I'm* the one who will be asking the questions here. Which painting are you talking about—and why do you think Cobb had it when he died?"

"I'm not sure which painting, but I think it's a Rembrandt. As for why I believe Cobb had it, that's privileged information."

"Fortune hunter, eh?" Reed scoffed. "You people are all alike."

I was tired of watching insecure men in positions of authority act like pricks.

"You don't know the first thing about me," I retorted. "I'm a licensed investigator who's acting on behalf of a client. A few months ago, I was nearly killed while uncovering an international gun smuggling operation. Now I might be close to finding a priceless work of art that's been missing for thirty-five years, something *your* agency has been unable to produce itself during that whole time. Are we going to help each other or not?"

Reed sized me up, and his tone softened.

"You know I can't share any specifics about an ongoing investigation."

"Of course."

"But we've suspected for years that someone from the Leone crime family in Boston was behind the heist. That's all I can divulge right now. This cooperation goes both ways, though. You have to help me as well. Anything you find that could lead to a break in the case and the return of the other missing works, I want to know."

* * *

After leaving the FBI building, I proceeded to the Isabella Stewart Gardner Museum in Boston, which was only a few hundred yards down the street from the Museum of Fine Arts. Although I'd attended college at UMass Boston and had been to the MFA many times, somehow I had never been to the Gardner Museum before.

I parked in the MFA parking garage on Huntington Avenue and walked the two blocks to the Gardner Museum. I had an appointment to see Lauren Toews, a curator at the museum, at eleven thirty.

The museum consists of an older main building and a more

recent addition featuring a stunning glass façade, constructed well after the 1990 heist. Ms. Toews met me in the lobby of the main building. She was a tall, elegantly-dressed Black woman wearing tortoise shell glasses and a matching rust-colored skirt and jacket.

She greeted me with nearly the same words that Special Agent Reed had spoken, but with a wholly different tone: Whereas Reed had seemed bored, even condescending, when asking me about the claim I'd made in setting up the meeting, Toews appeared delighted.

"That's correct. I think I know who might have possessed one of the stolen Rembrandts before he died," I repeated, "but I don't know where it's being kept. I'm hoping you can help me find it."

"Well, that's the best news I've heard in quite some time," she enthused. "I'll certainly try to help if I can."

As she led me to the Dutch Room, where the Rembrandts were displayed before they were stolen, I told her about Walter Cobb and his journal entries. The missing paintings' frames still hung on the walls, the empty spaces where the artwork had appeared serving as a jarring reminder of their theft.

"Do you know if Cobb was somehow connected to the museum?" I asked. "I'm trying to figure out how one of the stolen Rembrandts might have ended up in his possession."

"I've never heard his name before. But I'll double-check to see if he's in our records anywhere."

"Cobb was a collector of rare artifacts from around the world. He was also fastidious, disciplined, and highly organized. I know I'm putting you on the spot by asking this, but without knowing anything else about his habits, what's your best guess about what he might have done with a stolen Rembrandt?

What would *you* do with it?"

Toews considered my question.

"Like you said, I don't really know anything about him. But there are only two reasons a collector would acquire a valuable piece like that: either to sell it for a profit or enjoy it for themselves."

"I'm pretty sure he didn't sell it," I said. "He wrote in his journal that he was devising a way to 'stow it away secretly.' Nearly three months later, there was another journal entry suggesting he was successful. And besides, nowhere is his journal does he describe selling any items, only acquiring them."

"Then he acquired it so that he could look at it. I highly doubt the painting is stashed away in some closet or foot locker somewhere. My guess is it's hanging on a wall within some secret room or hideaway."

* * *

When I got home from Boston, I took Minerva for another walk around the block. Then I sat down in front of my laptop to check my email.

Amid the usual spam mail offers, there was welcome message from the Kingdom of Light Church that included a PDF of the church directory.

With the same thrill of anticipation that the journalist Geraldo Rivera must have felt in the 1980s when he was about to open Al Capone's vault, I clicked on the file and perused the document. (Though I hoped for better results than Geraldo had during his live TV special that revealed nothing but an empty safe to millions of viewers.)

On the first page of the directory was a listing of church officers and employees. I noticed that Charlie Dawes was listed as the sexton, responsible for building maintenance. *A sexton named Charlie?* I mused. *Ain't this some congregation...*

As the church sexton, it wouldn't have been strange for Dawes to be in the building when I was watching Keefe a few days earlier. Just as it wasn't unusual for Ackerman to have been there that morning, either.

I scanned the list of members for anyone with the initials "RA." There were two possibilities: Robert Allen of Concord and Raymond Amendola of Pembroke.

Searching for information about the two men online, I learned that Robert Allen was twenty-nine and worked as an electrician. He owned a cherry-red Dodge Challenger. I couldn't find a current photo of him on the Internet; his social media profile pictures were just thumbnail photos of Happy Gilmore swinging a golf club. However, his social media posts suggested that he enjoyed watching NASCAR races, and many of his posts featured photos of muscle cars.

Raymond Amendola was thirty-seven years old and worked for a hardware store. He was married and drove an early-model Chevy Silverado pickup truck. That was the extent of what I was able to learn about him online, as he wasn't on social media—and I couldn't find any photos of him, either.

The fact that Robert Allen liked fast cars fit the traditional profile of someone who was a wheel man in an illegal enterprise. But it wasn't definitive proof that he was the "RA" mentioned in the Project Abaddon document—especially since I had no idea whether Raymond Amendola possessed similar skills or interests. For all I knew, Amendola could have been undefeated in back roads drag racing contests going back to his high school days.

I also scanned the church directory for Trace Gladstone's

name, but he wasn't listed. Nor did I find anyone with a name resembling "Trig."

That was all I was able to glean from the directory.

Not Geraldo-level futility. But not nearly conclusive, either.

* * *

Later that afternoon, I called Peter Bowles. I wanted to know how thoroughly he'd searched Cobb's house for some type of hidden artifact after he read those journal entries—and whether he'd looked for any secret rooms or compartments.

"When I read Cobb's journal, that was the first thought I had as well," he said. "I looked for a secret room, but I didn't find anything like that."

"What's happening with the house now? Is it empty? Has it been sold?"

"I'm still liquidating Cobb's possessions. You're welcome to come look for yourself. I'm at the house now, as a matter of fact."

The drive from Manchester to nearby Bedford took only a few minutes, and by three o'clock I was parked in the circular driveway of the Cobb family estate.

The house itself was a rambling mansion with twenty-three rooms, including six bathrooms. Bowles met me on the front porch and led me inside the cavernous foyer. "Holler if you need anything," he said.

I wasn't sure I had the lung capacity to holler that loud.

It took me more than two hours to examine every seam in every wall, tapping with a croquet mallet as I went to determine if any of the walls sounded hollow. Satisfied that I wasn't missing any hidden chambers within the structure, I found Bowles in a downstairs study organizing some of Cobb's remaining antiques.

"Any luck?" he asked.

"Nope. I'm all tapped out."

* * *

After returning home for dinner, I decided to watch the Bruins' season opener at the Tipsy Moose.

When I got there, Kris was already seated at the bar. Amalia was busy making a round of margaritas for the cocktail waitress, and Kris was engaged in a conversation with the guy sitting to her left. It sounded like they were debating which episode of the TV show *Community* was the most creative.

"Have you seen the show?" Kris asked me as I settled into the stool to her right.

"Only the first few episodes. The Joel McHale character kinda bugged me. But let me guess: It's about a diverse group of students who come together as a community as they learn more about each other and realize their similarities outweigh their differences."

"Well, yeah. That's the essence. But it's so much more than that."

The guy to Kris's left was wearing a Brad Marchand Bruins jersey, despite the fact that Marchand no longer played for the team. He had shaggy brown hair and a patch of wispy hair on his chin.

"Not only did the show explore what it means to be part of a community," he rhapsodized, "but it also played around with storytelling conventions. There was a paintball episode that was an homage to *Die Hard*, and a claymation episode in the style of a Rankin/Bass Christmas special, and an entire episode that was just a game of *Dungeons & Dragons*."

"That does sound pretty creative," I conceded. "Maybe I should give it another try."

The conversation about the TV show ended once the puck dropped and the Bruins game was under way.

Experiencing a game with other people is so much more enjoyable than watching it alone. Every rush of the puck up the ice, every jarring hit along the boards, every near miss with a blistering shot on goal elicits "oohs" and "aahs" that energize the entire room and lift the collective soul of viewers.

Maybe it was all the talk about that television series when I arrived. But I couldn't help thinking how the people watching the game in that bar that night were a community, and how rooting for the same team draws together such a widely disparate group of people—business people and bricklayers, politicians and plumbers—binding them to each other like the nylon cord that attaches a hockey net to its goal posts.

The Bruins got great goaltending from their starting goalie, but they found themselves losing to the New York Rangers, 1-0, heading into the third period. They hadn't had many high-quality scoring chances throughout the game, and so they changed up their strategy in the game's final period by shooting the puck at the net every chance they got and hoping for a tipped puck or rebound. Volume over quality.

I found that investigative work was often like that. When you're not having success in being more strategic, sometimes just throwing stuff at the wall and hoping for a break is your only option.

That's what I'd done in talking with Davis Reed from the FBI and Lauren Toews from the Gardner Museum earlier that day. I didn't have any solid leads in finding the stolen Rembrandt for Peter Bowles, and so I took a wild shot in traveling to Boston and talking with professionals who had intimate knowledge about the theft. Unfortunately, I wasn't successful.

It didn't work for the Bruins that night, either, as they failed to score in the third period and the game was decided by that same 1-0 margin.

Better luck next time.

Chapter 12

The meetings with Special Agent Davis Reed of the FBI and Lauren Toews from the Gardner Museum didn't reveal much more about the heist than I already knew. What I needed to learn was how one of the missing Rembrandts ended up in Cobb's possession after the robbery—and what he did with it thereafter.

Based on the research I'd done so far, there was no suggestion that Cobb was directly linked to Boston's organized crime world. More likely, he had acquired the Rembrandt through an intermediary.

The entries in Cobb's journal referred to three different art brokers he'd used over the years to build his collection of works. Maybe one of those three brokers was also the person who'd helped him acquire the stolen Rembrandt? If that was the case, it seemed likely that whoever had connected Cobb with the painting also had ties to either the Gardner Museum or the Boston mafia.

The three names I had from the journal were Mae Ling, N.C. Clarke, and Laverne Pemberton. After breakfast on Thursday morning, I sat down at my laptop, called up my '90s playlist—which had left off at Shawn Colvin's terrific cover of the Warren Zevon song "Tenderness on the Block"—and set out to find a possible connection between these three art brokers and either the museum or the Leone crime family.

Mae Ling, I learned, was a New York City-based classical pianist and one of the world's foremost experts on ancient musical instruments. That made sense, as her name only appeared in the journal whenever Cobb had acquired a rare musical artifact. It seemed unlikely that she would have anything to do with helping Cobb purchase a Baroque-era painting.

N.C. Clarke was a jack-of-all-trades art broker from Oak Park, Illinois. He'd been a former curator for the Chicago Museum of Art, and he seemed to know a little bit about all kinds of curios—including paintings from masters and obscure artists alike.

Oak Park, I knew, was a geographical point of convergence where two giants of modern art and literature—the architect Frank Lloyd Wright and the novelist Ernest Hemingway—both lived at the same time for about a decade.

Wright had maintained a home and studio on Chicago Avenue in Oak Park for ten years when Hemingway was born and raised on North Oak Park Avenue, less than half a mile away. Wright left the small city in 1911, when Hemingway was just a boy of eleven or twelve. But I'd always found it fascinating that two of the most creative and ingenious minds in history had resided within four blocks of each other for a brief period—and I liked to think that maybe the young Hemingway delivered Wright's newspaper or had some other encounter with the architectural luminary during the time they shared there.

However, this historical footnote was of no use in helping me find Cobb's missing painting. And a thorough Internet search revealed no obvious connection between N.C. Clarke and either organized crime or the Gardner Museum.

Laverne Pemberton lived in Andover, Massachusetts. She had majored in art history at Columbia University, and after working as a curator for several museums up and down the East Coast, she'd struck out on her own as an art broker. The curriculum vitae on her website revealed that she'd helped broker art sales for numerous institutions … including the Isabella Stewart Garner Museum in Boston.

Score!!!

Ms. Pemberton had clear connections to both the Gardner Museum *and* Walter Cobb. I was willing to bet she had been the go-between who'd brought together Cobb and the person who'd either stolen the Rembrandt from the museum or ended up with it after the heist.

Now, it was time to see what she might know about the missing painting's location.

I called Ms. Pemberton, and she agreed to talk with me at her Andover home later that morning.

* * *

Laverne Pemberton lived in a large, colonial-style house surrounded by a white picket fence. She was an elderly woman with long gray hair tied up in a bun. She wore a chartreuse-colored blouse and black silk pants, and a pair of reading glasses hung from a silver chain around her neck.

She greeted me pleasantly and led me through her house to the back patio, where we sat at a wrought-iron table with an intricate flower design. A teapot, two porcelain cups and saucers, and a bowl with a variety of herbal teas were laid out on the table.

"Help yourself to some tea," she offered.

Her backyard was beautifully landscaped, featuring a garden bursting with fall colors: chrysanthemums and daisies and several kinds of flowers I didn't recognize.

"Did you plant those yourself?" I asked as I chose an orange pekoe teabag from the bowl.

"Yes, I did. Now that I'm retired, I spend most of my time tending to my garden. Now, how can I help you?"

"When you were working, I understand you served as a broker for the Gardner Museum."

"Yes, on occasion. They have their own curators who are wonderful at what they do. But sometimes, acquiring rare pieces can be challenging—and they would bring me in as a consultant to help close the deal."

"You also served as a broker for Walter Cobb. What was he like to work with?"

"Oh yes. Walter." Ms. Pemberton paused to reflect. "A nice man, very polite. Not much of a talker, but he had a real appreciation for art."

"Were you aware that he passed away?"

"No, I hadn't heard. That's very sad. How do you know him?"

"I work for an agent of his estate, and I'm trying to find a piece I believe he acquired from you. I'm hoping you can help me."

"Sure, if I can. What's the item?"

I hesitated, unsure of how to proceed. "It's a Rembrandt. I believe it might be one of the items taken from the Gardner Museum thirty-five years ago."

Ms. Pemberton didn't flinch. "You think Walter Cobb has one of the stolen works? What makes you think that?"

"It's a long story."

"And you think *I'm* the person who brokered the sale? Good heavens, no."

"Ms. Pemberton, you don't have to worry about getting into legal trouble. I'm not interested in bringing anyone to justice. And besides, I think the statute of limitations in that crime has expired, anyway. I'm just trying to find the painting."

Laverne took a sip of her tea, and her hand was perfectly steady and she raised the cup to her lips. "Well, I'm sorry I can't be more helpful. Would you care for some more tea before you go?"

* * *

Ms. Pemberton's demeanor had seemed as calm as the Merrimack River on a windless day in August. But I couldn't help thinking she was lying.

Despite my suspicion, I felt it was time to shift gears and focus again on the Project Abaddon case. I was keenly aware that the "final prep" for whatever the plot's perpetrators had planned was exactly one week away—and I was still no closer to uncovering the truth than I was when I first learned of the document's existence.

Instead of returning to my apartment, I drove on up to Concord to talk with Katrina McAdoo, Trace Gladstone's ex-wife.

Katrina worked as a hairdresser at a salon on Loudon Road. Business was slow at the salon that morning, and she wasn't busy with a client when I walked in. Neither was her coworker, and the two women were talking about the challenges of raising a teenage daughter as I approached them.

"Ms. McAdoo? My name is Parker Hanson. I'm a detective, and I'm hoping I can talk with you about your ex-husband."

She rolled her eyes and shrugged at her colleague, as if to

say, "I'm sorry." Then she gestured wordlessly toward a room in the back of the salon, and I followed her there.

The break room contained a counter with a sink and a microwave oven, as well as a wooden banquet-style table surrounded by metal folding chairs. Katrina squeezed her copious frame into a chair, and I joined her at the table.

She tapped a cigarette from a pack of Newport 100s, lit it, and blew a stream of smoke from her nose. "He in trouble again?" she inquired.

"You tell me. I found the note you wrote to him the other day."

I didn't say any more. I was hoping she might assume that I knew what the note was about and talk freely about it, thereby revealing its true nature. If I just came out and asked her what it meant, she might clam up altogether.

"You—you know about that?" she stammered.

I nodded and waited for her to continue.

"Obviously things have been hard since Trace went to jail," she said, taking a long drag of her cigarette.

"Of course."

"Is there something you want to ask me?" she asked, clearly bored with the conversation.

"How did you know what Trace was planning to do?"

"He called me up and told me. Said I deserved to know."

"And how did you feel when he told you?"

"You saw the note," she retorted. "What do *you* think?"

Point taken. "Why do you think he might do it?" I asked, still fishing blindly.

She looked at me suspiciously. "If you're accusing my ex of a crime," she said, stubbing out her cigarette, "I got nothing else to say. My break is over."

"But you don't have any clients right now," I noted.

"Thanks for reminding me. Have a good day."

* * *

I'd gotten nowhere with Katrina McAdoo. Now it was time to try Gladstone himself.

I stopped at a sandwich shop for a veggie wrap and a sugar-free iced tea, then resumed my stakeout of his trailer.

It was just after one p.m. when I arrived, and I stayed until nearly eight at night. Not once in those seven hours did Gladstone emerge. I returned home, walked and fed Minerva, and waited for Callie to come over after work.

On Friday morning, I was back at it. Callie agreed to stay with Minerva until her dance classes began, and I was parked down the road from Gladstone's trailer by ten thirty.

Nothing happened until four o'clock in the afternoon, when he finally came out of his trailer carrying a navy blue backpack. He tossed the bag in the back seat, got into his car, and drove off.

I followed Gladstone as he drove along Route 3. He turned into Blossom Hill Cemetery, and I crept along several hundred yards behind as he zigzagged down the property's narrow lanes. From a distance, I saw him park his El Camino at the very back of the cemetery, along the westernmost lane running parallel to Route 3.

I pulled over at a safe distance and got out of my car, pretending to pay my respects at a grave site while I watched him exit his vehicle. He grabbed his knapsack from the back seat and deftly slung it onto his back. Then he disappeared into the trees behind the cemetery, following a trail head that I hadn't noticed before.

I wasn't familiar with the trails in that location. I called up

Google Maps on my phone, and I saw that Penacook Lake lay beyond those woods, about a mile from the cemetery.

Penacook Lake served as the main water supply for the city of Concord. The lake was off limits to swimming, boating, fishing, or any other recreational activity, and barbed wire fencing protected it from public access along the roads that formed a half circle around its northern, western, and southern shores.

Yet, I had no idea whether a similar barrier shielded the lake's eastern shore—the one Gladstone was heading towards at that very moment. The eastern shore wasn't accessible by car ... but maybe it could be approached by trail.

Was Gladstone's destination the lake? I wondered. *Could Project Abaddon involve poisoning the water supply for an entire city?*

A powerful sense of dread formed in my chest and slowly settled into my stomach—and I sprinted toward the trail head to follow him.

* * *

As I entered the forest, I thought: *Am I crazy?*

If Gladstone was, indeed, on his way to poison the city's water supply, I didn't know what I would be able to do about it. What were the odds that, alone and unarmed, I could stop a former Navy SEAL with my bare hands—someone who'd actually killed another guy in a bar fight eight years earlier?

On the other hand, I couldn't just stand by and do nothing. And if I waited for backup to arrive before setting off in pursuit of Gladstone, I would have no idea where he'd ended up within the hundreds of acres of wilderness behind the cemetery.

So I pressed on through the forest, trying not to lose Gladstone while treading carefully to avoid the sound of leaves crunching underfoot—my heart laboring like a jackhammer as I worried that he might double back and catch me.

The canopy of trees overhead served as a filter that diffused the late afternoon sunshine, bathing the forest in an eerie glow. Southern New Hampshire still hadn't experienced a frost yet, and I tried to ignore the incessant buzzing of mosquitoes swarming around my head as I focused on tracing the steps that Gladstone had taken.

About half a mile into the woods, the trees began to thin. At the same time, the trail wended its way around massive piles of roughly cut granite blocks. It appeared we'd reached the site of an old stone quarry.

As I rounded a bend in the trail, I saw that Gladstone had taken a short side spur that led to a large outcropping of rock. He was standing atop the rock, completely still—his lean body silhouetted against the darkening sky.

I watched him in silence, curious about what he was doing.

Without a word, Gladstone raised his arms to the heavens. Then he toppled forward and disappeared from view.

A second or two later, I heard the smack of his body colliding with water—and the sound of a giant *splash* echoed through the forest.

* * *

I stood rooted in place for a moment, my mind trying to process what I'd just witnessed. Then I ran forward to the spot where Gladstone had been standing.

I found myself on a ledge overlooking a deep quarry shaft, maybe a hundred yards in diameter. Nearly forty feet below me, ripples were radiating from where Gladstone had plunged into the brackish water.

I waited for him to surface, but there was no sign of his body. Fifteen seconds passed, then thirty...

I realized I had been completely wrong about Gladstone and his intentions. He hadn't been heading for Penacook Lake.

He was trying to kill himself.

The backpack that Gladstone was carrying wasn't filled with poisonous chemicals. It was ballast meant to pull him beneath the surface of the water in this desolate, abandoned quarry.

Maybe it wasn't my place to interfere. If that's what Gladstone wanted, who was I to change the course of his fate?

But that's not how I'm wired. I wasn't about to just watch someone die. And besides, the chances were pretty high that Gladstone wasn't in a healthy enough frame of mind to know what he wanted at that time.

Acting partly on instinct and partly on adrenaline, I kicked off my sneakers. I peeled off the UMass Boston sweatshirt I was wearing and stepped out of my jeans.

Then, without another thought, I jumped into the murky water below.

Chapter 13

I seemed to fall for an eternity, the air rushing past me in a scream.

I hadn't stopped to consider what I was doing, and it was only on the way down that I wondered if the water was deep enough for me not to be seriously injured … or worse.

But it was too late to change course now—and I braced for the impact of the water's surface.

The cold hit me like a punch, nearly causing me to gasp, but somehow I held on to the air inside my lungs. I forced my eyes open, desperately searching the murky green depths beneath me.

A shadow appeared in my field of vision. It was Gladstone. But his body looked lifeless, his limbs suspended motionless in the water—and he was slowly sinking.

I kicked downward, my arms flailing and my lungs burning. My fingers brushed fabric, then grabbed hold of his arm. But with the backpack on, he was too heavy to pull toward the surface.

I struggled with the pack, trying to yank it free. But the straps kept snagging on the denim of his jacket. Panic clawed at me, until finally the pack broke free and sank to the bottom.

With clumsy strokes, I pulled Gladstone upward. My chest

screamed for air. Then, at last, we broke the surface. Coughing and sputtering, I managed to drag him onto the rocks at the water's edge.

I lay motionless for a few seconds, taking in huge lungfuls of air while I regained my breath. Then I sat upright and started performing CPR on Gladstone, hoping to revive him.

The chest compressions forced the water from his lungs. Remarkably, he started breathing on his own after a few minutes.

Once he was breathing, I scrambled up the rocks to the cliff overlooking the water. With darkness rapidly enshrouding the forest, I retrieved my cell phone from the pocket of my jeans and dialed 911.

***

Forty-five minutes later, I was sitting in the back of an ambulance, wrapped in a wool blanket as we sped toward Concord Hospital. An EMT was tending to Gladstone, who lay prone on a stretcher beside me.

"Is he going to be okay?" I asked.

"Too early to tell. But if he does pull through, he owes his life to you. Your instincts were spot on in taking care of him until we got there."

While I'd waited for the paramedics to arrive, I'd applied the skills I had learned in Scouting as a youth. I'd built a fire for warmth and stripped off the wet clothes from Gladstone's body to prevent hypothermia from setting in. I'd amassed a bed of pine needles next to the fire for insulation, and I'd lain Gladstone's body on this improvised bed. I'd torn my sweatshirt into two pieces and used one of the pieces to cover Gladstone, while I kept myself warm with the other one.

At the hospital, I remained in the emergency room until

my body temperature returned to normal and a doctor pronounced me fit to leave. Callie had gotten there as soon as her dance classes were over—I'd texted her about what happened and told her there was no need to rush to the ER, as I wasn't in any danger—and she brought me home and made me a bowl of chicken tortellini soup.

"You could have been killed," Callie whispered as we huddled together on the couch.

"Yeah, for like the fifth time in the last four months. Is there a 'frequently escapes death' club I can join, where the next one earns me a free beverage?"

She ignored my attempt at humor. "You're feeling okay now?"

"I guess so. But I'm not sure if the ER doctor did a good enough job in checking me out before discharging me. Wanna take a look?"

"Well," she replied, nimbly untying the drawstring on my sweatpants, "I suppose we should be thorough..."

* * *

Callie spent the night at my apartment, but she had to be in Portland, Maine, the next morning for a dance team competition involving her students. On her way home to shower and change, she dropped me off at the cemetery in Concord so I could retrieve my car.

As I was returning to my apartment, I ran into Amalia in the downstairs lobby. When I told her about my adventure the previous evening, she became somber.

"I'm glad you're okay," she said, giving me a hug. "What you did was very brave. You know, the suicide rate among veterans is double the rate of the general population—and an average of seventeen veterans commit suicide every day."

"Really? That's terrible. I had no idea."

"Yes. Many veterans have a tough time transitioning from the military to civilian life. They're used to a tight-knit community in the military, and when they don't have that 'brotherhood' anymore, it can be very isolating. I volunteer for a hotline that counsels vets who are having suicidal thoughts, and I hear it all the time."

"Gladstone's circumstances must have put him at even more risk. I can't imagine living with the guilt of killing someone accidentally in a drunken bar fight." I told Amalia about his back story.

"He was a SEAL, huh?" she said, looking pensive. I wondered if she felt a connection with him because of their shared experience in the special forces.

"I'm going back to the hospital later this morning to check on his condition," I told her, "and I have a few questions I'd like to ask him if he's up to responding. Want to come with me?"

"Yes, thanks. I'd like that."

* * *

Gladstone was in a private room on the hospital's second floor. He was fully awake when Amalia and I entered the room.

I introduced us and asked how he was feeling.

"Hanson ... You the guy who saved me?" he asked.

"I am. I hope that's okay. But I couldn't just watch you die."

Gladstone squeezed his eyes shut. "Be better if I did. I'm a coward."

"Bullshit," Amalia said. She sat on the edge of Gladstone's bed and took his hand in her own. "You were a SEAL. There's nothing weak about that."

"What's more cowardly than taking your own life?" Gladstone retorted.

"You're in a bad place right now," she countered. "I'm sorry you're feeling that way. Dealing with strong emotions can be ten times harder than facing an enemy on the battlefield. But you're not alone. So many people just as tough as you are going through the same thing."

"Amalia's a former Ranger," I said. "She also counsels other veterans who are struggling with depression."

Gladstone opened his eyes, looked at her, and smiled. "Ranger, huh? Worried you wouldn't be able to cut it in the big leagues?"

"Whatever, Hollywood."

"You're looking good, Trace," I said, deflecting the good-natured ribbing between service branches before it devolved into a more heated rivalry. "Have the doctors said when you might be able to go home?"

"Probably tomorrow. Hey, what were you doing in those woods last night, anyway?"

"Following you, actually."

"Why would you do that?"

"I thought you might be planning some kind of attack with members of the Kingdom of Light Church. Are you?"

He didn't hesitate or show any signs that he might be lying. "I don't know what you're talking about."

"So you've never heard of Project Abaddon?"

"No. What's that?"

Ignoring his question, I asked him: "How is it that you know Jonah Keefe, and why were you meeting with him at the Barley House Restaurant last week?"

"The VA put me in touch with Reverend Keefe when I told them I felt alone and needed someone to talk to. But all he wanted to talk about was God and the church. I'm not into all that religious stuff."

"You should call the organization I volunteer for when you get home," Amalia said, giving him a card. "They'll help you without trying to recruit you into their group. And I wrote my own number on the back as well. If you ever feel so desperate that you want to end it all again, you can call me any time—day or night."

As we were leaving the hospital room, Gladstone called out: "Hey, thanks for jumping in the water to save me."

"No problem," I said, turning around to give him a "thumbs up" sign. "Just be grateful I know how to swim."

* * *

When I got home from the hospital, I took Minerva for a walk down to Veteran's Memorial Park, where I played fetch with her using a stick.

Though I was acting playful outwardly, my mind wouldn't let go of what happened the night before—like Minerva with a brand-new chew toy.

Gladstone missed the sense of community he felt in the armed forces, an absence he hadn't been able to replace in his life. It was one of the key factors that had driven him to attempt suicide as I watched. Perhaps not surprising, as we all need community to survive.

Jonah Keefe had tried to get Gladstone to join his community at the Kingdom of Light Church. Maybe Keefe genuinely cared about Gladstone's well-being. But I'd listened to his sermons, and so far I hadn't heard much of anything about the love and acceptance I'd always thought Christianity was supposed to espouse. That led me to believe Keefe had more self-serving motives in mind.

Gladstone needed a genuine friend. And Keefe appeared to have taken advantage of his vulnerability by trying to recruit him into the church.

The thought made me so angry that I felt like my organs were liquifying.

As for my inquiries into Project Abaddon, I'd just wasted nearly a full week in following Gladstone around, and I'd been completely wrong in suspecting he was part of a murderous plot. Now, with the "final prep" date rapidly approaching, I was back to square one in my investigation.

If I could just look inside Keefe's office at the church, I might finally discover the nature of this supposed attack. Maybe I'd have another chance to do so at the next day's service.

And maybe I could also learn who Robert Allen and Raymond Amendola were—and which of the two men was most likely to be the "RA" referred to in the document that P.J. Warner had discovered.

Chapter 14

At nine fifty-five the next morning, I was sitting in the same pew at the Kingdom of Light Church that I'd occupied the previous week. Once again, Chief Dalton Keane sat beside me.

"Sorry to bother you, Chief," I said, "but I'm still trying to learn everyone's name. Can you show me who Robert Allen is?"

Keane pointed to a young man sitting about ten rows from the front of the church. He had short, dark hair parted on the side, and he was wearing a navy blue golf pullover.

"And Raymond Amendola?"

Keane looked at me sideways.

"Are we going through the whole congregation alphabetically?"

"No sir, this is the last one."

He pointed out a slightly older guy with a thick mustache and hair the color of beach sand. Amendola was wearing a tartan-patterned, blue-and-gray flannel shirt, and he was sitting a few rows in front of Keane and me.

"Thanks. I appreciate it."

When the organist finished playing her prelude, Livy Keefe stood before the congregation and made her announcements.

"…And finally, our sexton, Charlie Dawes, is looking for volunteers to help him paint some of the church's interior spaces this Tuesday," she concluded. "There will be a sign-up sheet posted downstairs in the coffee area."

If I volunteer to help paint the church on Tuesday, I thought, *I might have a chance to look inside Jonah Keefe's office.*

I resolved to sign up once the service ended.

Jonah's sermon that morning focused on the many miracles performed by Jesus, such as Jesus's walking on water and Peter's miraculous catch of fish. In a strange convergence of the two cases I was working on, one of the miracles that Keefe talked about was Jesus calming the storm in the Gospel of Matthew—which also happened to be the subject of Rembrandt's *Christ in the Storm on the Sea of Galilee*.

Typical of what I'd come to expect from him, however, Keefe couched these miracles not in terms of wonder, but as something for sinners to dread. Again, he rattled off a long list of groups who should fear God's all-encompassing power—starting with nonbelievers.

When the service was over, I stood up and shuffled toward the top of the stairs like a condemned prisoner, joylessly making my way down to coffee hour with the other parishioners.

I had a job to do. But I didn't relish the thought of spending one more minute in that building than I had to.

As I'd listened to Keefe's sermon, I recalled the train of thought I'd had in the Tipsy Moose earlier that week about what makes a community. So many people turn to religion and churches as a way to find connection with other people. But a community can be either inclusive or exclusive. That is, it can welcome and value everyone, or it can restrict membership only to people who fit certain characteristics.

On its website, the Kingdom of Light Church said it welcomed everyone. But in practice, it established a very clear set of criteria for who belonged—and anyone who didn't fit those standards was made to feel unholy and unloved by God. I found that to be a very toxic and manipulative dynamic.

On their surface, the church's members all seemed pleasant. But I was reminded of what someone once said about the difference between "nice" and "kind." Whereas the parishioners were outwardly polite, I wondered how much genuine kindness and empathy for their fellow human beings they possessed underneath.

As I joined the members for coffee hour, I felt as if I were punching a clock at the start of a twelve-hour shift in the mines. Yet, I hid my true feelings behind a pleasant façade, smiling and nodding at everyone who made eye contact.

How do spies spend years embedded among their enemies without going crazy, I wondered? I had only been in that environment for two consecutive Sundays, and already I felt a sourness in the pit of my stomach.

I got in line for coffee and refreshments, standing behind an elderly retired couple from Bow named Ernest and Louisa Hutchens.

"I always love hearing about Peter's miraculous catch of fish," Ernest was saying, "because it reminds me of fishing myself."

"Oh yeah? You like to fish? Where do you go?" I said politely.

As I was talking with Ernest, I followed the movements of the two men who could be "RA" across the room with my eyes, trying to keep track of whom they interacted with. When I reached the refreshments, I took an apple cider doughnut against my better judgment, figuring I owed myself a treat for what I was enduring.

"I go out on Lake Winnipesaukee at least once a week in the summer," Ernest replied, helping himself to a cup of black coffee. "There's nothing like the feeling when a smallmouth bass strikes your line, then jumps out of the water as it tries to spit out the hook. It's the best two minutes of excitement there is."

"Ernest, dear, I think you're forgetting about our yearly anniversary nights," Louisa said with an impish grin, and I laughed out loud. Though I wasn't particularly comfortable in that setting, I had to admit I wouldn't mind spending more time with the Hutchenses.

Robert Allen was standing in a corner of the room, engaged in a conversation with someone I didn't recognize: a well-built guy about six feet tall with spikey blond hair. Raymond Amendola was seated at a table with the Arsenaults and someone I assumed was his wife.

"Who's that muscular guy talking with Robert Allen?" I asked the Hutchenses.

"That's Danny Coffey," Louisa said.

"What do you know about him?"

"From what I understand, he wanted to be a professional wrestler. He tried out for the WWE, but he didn't make the final cut. Now he works as a bouncer at a local bar."

"That's interesting. It must be pretty competitive to break into big-time wrestling. So, Ernest," I said, turning my attention back to Louisa's husband, "when you fish on Winnipesaukee, do you use your own boat?"

"I do. A twenty-two foot pontoon boat that I keep moored at the town docks in Meredith."

I was blinded by a sudden flash of light, as if someone had blasphemed in that very church and been struck by a bolt of lightning hurled by God himself.

Meredith is the name of a town in New Hampshire, I realized. *Maybe Walter Cobb was referring to the town in his journal, and not a person! I don't know why I didn't see it before.*

Ernest was saying something else to me, but I was no longer listening. My brain was reeling from the insight I'd just had, and I was far too excited to focus on anything else at the moment. All I wanted to do was get back in front of my computer and search the Internet for some connection between Cobb and the town of Meredith.

I knew it would be useless to continue probing the congregation for information about Project Abaddon while my mind was occupied elsewhere, so I excused myself and left.

Before exiting the church, I stopped at the table with the sign-up sheet and volunteered to help Charlie Dawes with his interior painting project later in the week. Then I hurried out of the building and bolted to my car, eager to learn where my brand-new line of inquiry on the location of the missing Rembrandt might take me.

My Honda Civic was parked between a plain white van on the left and a brick-red Ford Explorer on the right. As I approached the driver's side door of my car, I noticed that the person sitting in the passenger seat of the van—a young woman wearing a cream-colored blouse, with platinum blond hair piled high on top of her head—was sobbing.

Her window was down, and there was no one sitting beside her in the van's cab.

"I'm sorry to intrude, but is everything okay?" I asked her.

"No, it's not," she said softly. She looked up at me with frightened eyes, and a single tear streamed down her cheek. "But maybe you can help. What would *you* do if someone sent you this text?"

She held out her phone for me to read the message showing on the display.

As I leaned in to focus on the screen, I felt a sudden explosion of pain in my right temple, knocking me off balance.

I heard the van's side door open, and I was shoved from behind into the vehicle.

I landed belly-up on the floor of the van, feeling as helpless as an overturned beetle—watching the ceiling swirl around in a kaleidoscope of patterns as I heard the side door slam shut.

There was a flash of movement at my shoulder, and I heard the van's engine rumble to life.

A blurry figure appeared above me.

"We're taking a little drive now," the blur snickered, "and it'll be easier for all of us if you just relax and go along for the ride."

III

Faust and Furious

Chapter 15

s my head began to clear, I saw there were three other people in the van besides me.

The driver was a wiry Latino youth wearing a black warm-up jacket, black nylon sweatpants, and a thick gold chain around his neck. He was probably the guy who'd struck me in the head while my attention was fixed on the blond woman's phone, I realized.

The woman was still sitting in the passenger seat. She'd pulled on a plum leather jacket over her cream-colored blouse. The jacket matched the purple leather pants she was wearing. Her performance as a damsel in distress now over, she had stopped crying and was busy fixing her mascara using the mirror in the visor above her seat.

The third occupant was a hulk of a man crouched alongside me in the back of the vehicle. He was bald and had a squarish face, with eyes like tar pits and hands the size of goalie mitts. He was eating pistachios from a bag in his pocket and dropping the shells on the floor of the van.

The pistachio-eating giant had probably opened the van door from inside just as the driver assaulted me and shoved me in. I was lucky the two men's roles weren't reversed, as I might still be unconscious—or worse—if the big guy had slugged me instead.

Aside from the throbbing pain I felt in my head every time we hit a bump in the road, which was quite often given the condition of the pavement that had weathered many New England winters, the ride was brief and uneventful. No one said another word, and within ten minutes we were parked outside an unmarked building that looked like it might be a garage or a warehouse.

I stepped out of the van without being told when the bald-headed goliath opened the side door.

Standing there to greet me were two additional men. One was an older fellow of considerable girth. He looked to be in his late forties, with dark, slicked-back hair. He was wearing a brown suit with no tie, and the ripples of fat from his neck extended out over the collar of his shirt. When his suit coat flapped open in the breeze, I noticed a gun holstered on his right hip.

The other man was younger, maybe mid-thirties, and of average height and build. He was wearing a navy blue polo shirt, tan chinos, and loafers. He had curly brown hair and piercing blue eyes, with a few pockmarks on his cheeks that spoiled an otherwise handsome face. He appeared to be in charge, and the man in the brown suit was probably a bodyguard.

Were it not for the company he kept, the guy in the polo shirt could have been mistaken for a software coder, hedge fund manager, or sales rep at a multinational pharmaceutical firm.

We were joined by my companions from the van, and the leader spoke up.

"I apologize for the theatrics in bringing you here, Mr.

Hanson. But I felt it was urgent that we should meet."

Theatrics? Who was this guy? He was clearly linked to organized crime, though he didn't look or sound like a typical mobster.

"You could've just called me," I replied. "My number's on my website."

Ignoring my remark, he pointed to the blond woman who'd distracted me by pretending to be distressed. "This is Sal."

Sal blew a bubble with the gum she was chewing in response.

"Rico." He indicated the Latino youth in the black tracksuit, who nodded to me silently.

"Spiller." He pointed to the guy who'd been next to me in the van. The behemoth winked at me, and I wondered whether "Spiller" was his last name or a nickname—like a vivid description of what he did to the blood of people who crossed the gang, maybe?

"Nick the Neck," the leader said, gesturing to the man in the suit beside him, though it was pretty obvious whom he meant.

Nick just stood passively, acknowledging neither me nor his boss.

"And I'm Todd. Todd Primo."

Maybe I'd spent far too much time reading comic books as a child, but the motley cast of characters standing in front of me reminded me of a gang of cartoon supervillains, like the Fearsome Five or the Royal Flush Gang.

Yet, as amusing as that image was, it hadn't escaped my attention that I was in very real peril.

"My sources tell me you're looking for a certain painting," Primo said.

I waited for him to say something else. When he didn't, I spoke up.

"You seem to be well informed."

"I have eyes and ears all over the city."

"I'm sure you do." I wanted to get this meeting over with as quickly as possible, so I moved it along. "What's your interest in this object?"

Primo chuckled. "All business, I see. I like that." He took a handkerchief from his back pocket, wiped the corner of his eye, and put it back. "The item you're searching for went missing from an associate of mine, and he'd like it back. We'll pay you double what you stand to collect from your current arrangement."

I frowned. "That painting is stolen property. Are you saying your associate had something to do with its theft?"

"I'm not saying anything. You can make your own inferences."

Inferences? Was Primo a Harvard-educated gangster?

"How did your associate happen to lose the painting?" I asked him.

He stared at me for a moment. "What business is it of yours?"

"If I'm going to find it, that detail could be relevant."

"Are you saying we have a deal?"

No, we most certainly don't, I thought. But I wasn't about to say that to a crime boss.

"I'll have to think about it."

"Well, don't take too long." Primo took a business card from his wallet and handed it to me. "This is my direct line. Call me when you've decided. But while you're doing your thinking, I want you to remember my friends here and what they're capable of."

Sal blew another bubble with her gum. Spiller grinned and cracked his knuckles.

"Rico will drive you back to your car."

Primo turned to leave, then paused and turned back around. "Oh, and one more thing. When you call, don't mention the painting itself. The feds like to listen in on my conversations, and I let them think I don't know what they're up to. It's a little game we play."

Some game.

Personally, I preferred baseball or hockey.

* * *

When I got back to my apartment, I called Detective Connor and told him about my encounter with Todd Primo.

"Congratulations," Connor said. "You've just met Concord's biggest organized crime lord."

Gee, swell. What's my prize, a bullet to the back of my head?

"What can you tell me about him?"

"He runs the New Hampshire branch of the Leone crime syndicate in Boston. Smart guy, too. Has an MBA from Bentley."

"I didn't know the mob had such strict hiring standards."

"He grew up without a father, and from what I heard, one of his neighbors—a mid-level mob boss in charge of drug trafficking in Chelsea—took him under his wing. By the age of thirteen, Primo was working part-time as a mule to support his family. He earned a scholarship to college, probably figured he'd lead a normal life. But then his mentor got sick, and Primo ran the drug business for him on the side while finishing his MBA. He realized the stuff he was learning in grad school could revolutionize the syndicate's business. He streamlined the drug supply chain, saved the Leone crime family millions of dollars, and was put in charge of all of New Hampshire the following year."

121

"Just when I thought I was out, they pull me back in," I said, doing my best Al Pacino impersonation from *The Godfather, Part 3.*

"Yeah. Something like that. Why would he be interested in you?"

"You mean, aside from my sparkling personality?"

"Obviously."

I told Connor about the case I was working on for Peter Bowles and how Primo was connected. "So, are drugs and stolen art the Leone syndicate's main areas of focus, or do they have other hobbies as well?"

"Primo also controls the gun trafficking trade in the state. There's not an illegal weapon sold in New Hampshire that he doesn't know about. In fact, I'm willing to bet he was the source of those firearms your buddy Kyle Hammond was smuggling into Canada."

"If you know so much about his operations, why not just put him away?"

"Oh, sure. Simple as that. The city of Concord and the feds have been trying to pin something on him for years. We've actually been working with the FBI on a sting that involves Primo's acquisition of stolen diamonds from a South African courier—so you'd better stay out of the way."

"I'll take your advice."

"I mean it, Parker. Don't be fooled by his Joe College, finance bro image. Primo is a dangerous character—someone you don't want to be messing with."

* * *

Callie was coming over to my apartment in an hour, but I didn't have the energy to make us dinner. I figured we could get takeout from a local sushi place I liked.

Instead of prepping food, I sank into the sofa and turned on the TV.

The Bruins were tied with the Tampa Bay Lightning, 3-3, early in the third period of a Sunday matinee game at the Garden. I watched the rest of the game while my mind tried to process what just happened.

Someone in the Leone crime syndicate either was behind the Gardner Museum heist or had received the stolen artwork. That meshed with the information I'd gotten from Davis Reed, the FBI agent in Boston. Then, somehow, one of the Rembrandts taken from the museum had ended up in Walter Cobb's possession.

But *how?*

I was pretty sure Laverne Pemberton knew the answer. She hadn't been willing to talk before, but in light of my adventure that afternoon, I figured it was worth another try.

Primo was determined to retrieve the stolen painting that Cobb had taken ownership of. That painting was the museum's rightful property, and there was no way I was going to just hand it over to the syndicate. (Not if I had any choice in the matter, anyway.)

But if I declined Primo's request to find the painting on his behalf, I risked making an enemy out of him. I also had no doubt that Primo's goons would be shadowing me wherever I went, regardless of whether I agreed to work for him or not, and would probably try to take the painting by force if I discovered it.

With seven minutes left in the third period of the hockey game, Bruins forward David Pastrnak was hauled down as he tried to establish position in front of the Tampa Bay net, but no penalty was called.

Bruins defenseman Charlie McAvoy took on the role of enforcer for his team, challenging the guilty Lightning player to a brawl. McAvoy received a two-minute instigation penalty, and both players got five for fighting. The Lightning scored during the resulting power play, and that's how the game ended—4-3, Tampa Bay.

While I was frustrated by the outcome, I couldn't really blame McAvoy for the loss. He was just standing up for his teammate.

I turned off the TV with a sigh and thought about what I was going to do about Primo.

I wasn't about to tell Callie what happened that afternoon, because I didn't want to upset her. But there was someone I *could* talk to about my dilemma: Amalia.

Primo traveled with his own personal bodyguard, Nick the Neck.

Maybe it was time I had an enforcer on *my* side as well.

Chapter 16

The "final prep" date for Project Abaddon was in just a few days, and I still didn't know any of the plot's key details. However, I'd signed up to help paint the church on Tuesday morning, and I felt good about my chances of learning what I needed to know while volunteering. So on Monday, I decided to turn my attention back to the missing Rembrandt.

By ten o'clock that morning, I was sitting on Laverne Pemberton's back patio again, a cup of mint tea in my hand and a plate of butter cookies (which I was trying to ignore) within easy reach.

This time, Amalia was with me.

When I'd told Amalia about my encounter with Todd Primo and offered her a job as my personal protector on the Bowles case, she'd jumped at the chance for some extra excitement.

If I was right in suspecting that Ms. Pemberton had been the person to deliver the stolen Rembrandt to Cobb, then the last thing Laverne would want is to appear on the mob's radar. If Primo knew she was at least partly responsible for the painting's sale to another owner, I could only imagine how he and his goons might retaliate. As a result, I had gone to great lengths to make sure I wasn't being followed that morning.

I had driven into a parking garage in downtown Manchester, stashed my car on the third level, and taken the stairs up to level five, where Amalia was waiting for me in her jeep. I'd slipped into the jeep's back seat and crouched down on the floor. Fifteen minutes later, Amalia drove out of the garage, and we headed south to Ms. Pemberton's estate in Andover, Massachusetts.

"As I told you before, Detective, I don't know anything about those stolen works from the Gardner Museum," Ms. Pemberton was saying as she poured herself a cup of tea from the kettle on the wrought-iron table in front of us. "I really don't know how I can help you."

"You don't have to call me Detective, Laverne. I'm not on the police force, and this is just an informal conversation. Just three people talking. You have my word that nothing you say will be repeated to anyone else."

"But I don't *have* anything to say."

I shifted in my seat.

"Here's what I already know, Laverne. I've confirmed from two separate sources that a member of the Leone crime family in Boston possessed at least one, and maybe all, of the items stolen from the museum in the spring of 1990. I also learned that one of these works went missing shortly after the robbery. I'd be willing to stake my entire professional reputation that it ended up with Walter Cobb and that *you* were the broker. I'm just trying to fill in the missing pieces. Who was the seller, and how did that person end up with the painting? Do you have any idea what Cobb did with the Rembrandt once he got ahold of it or where it might be now?"

"Ms. Pemberton, you have a beautiful garden," Amalia chimed in, indicating the rows of color behind us. "My mother loved flowers, too. When we immigrated to New England from El Salvador, she was fascinated by the variety of wildflowers she'd never seen before. She planted purple dome asters, black-eyed Susans, and blazing star in our front yard. She wanted the whole neighborhood to be able to enjoy them. She would tell me: *Beautiful things are meant to be seen.*"

"That's right," I added, picking up where Mal left off. "The world deserves to see a masterpiece like *Christ in the Storm on the Sea of Galilee* again. In your heart, I think you agree. Help us find the painting, so it can be enjoyed by everyone."

Tears formed in Laverne's eyes, and she took a moment to compose herself.

"You were right about Walter Cobb acquiring one of the stolen paintings and my role in brokering the deal," she said at last. "But if the mob ever found out..."

"They won't. I promise."

Another pause.

"Okay," she said softly. "I'll tell you what I know. But I doubt if it will help you find the painting."

She took a sip of her tea, then added: "And by the way, it's not *Christ in the Storm on the Sea of Galilee* that Walter Cobb acquired. It's *A Lady and Gentleman in Black.*"

* * *

"As I told you when you first visited me, I used to serve as a broker for the Gardner Museum when they needed help in negotiating difficult acquisitions," Laverne began. "One of the curators I worked with there was a gentleman named Rudolph Aiken the third. He was a lovely man, with a sharp eye for detail and a real admiration for the masters. However, I heard he developed a gambling problem. He became a liability for the museum, and he was dismissed a few years before the heist.

"Of course, when the theft occurred, I was just as shocked as everyone else. Even more so when I got a call from Rudy about three weeks later. I hadn't spoken with him since he left the museum's employ. He sounded tense, and he asked if we could meet to discuss an important matter. I agreed to have lunch with him at a restaurant on Huntington Avenue we'd both dined at before.

"When I got to the restaurant, Rudy was already sitting at a private table in the back. I'll never forget the image I had of him that day: He was sipping Frangelico on the rocks and looking like that kid in the back of the class who'd just hit the teacher with a spitball. I joined him in the booth, and he told me the most remarkable tale.

"He said he owed nearly forty-eight thousand dollars to an organized crime syndicate, one of whose members happened to be behind the Gardner Museum theft. The mob had a connection to someone who could fence the stolen works, but they needed the advice of an art expert to safely store and preserve the items while they waited for the chance to sell them. They knew that Rudy had been a curator and offered to forgive some of his debt if he would help them.

"Rudy told me he accompanied a mob associate to a warehouse in Saugus, where the stolen items were being kept. He said he carefully examined the condition of each item, and having such valuable treasures in his hands gave him an unimaginable thrill. He recommended that they be moved to a climate-controlled environment to prevent cracking, warping, and mold growth as quickly as possible.

"The mob apparently arranged to have the stolen works transferred to the wine cellar of a restaurant that served as a front for its operations, though Rudy didn't tell me the name of the restaurant or where it was located. The wine cellar was no longer in use, so it could be set to the precise temperature and humidity needed to store the paintings safely.

"For some reason, they let Rudy oversee the process—and when all the works had been moved, he found himself alone with the stolen paintings in the wine cellar for a moment. I guess he was struck by a sudden idea for how he could pay back the mob once and for all—while also netting a handsome sum for his retirement."

"He stole from the mob to pay back the mob?" I asked in amazement.

"Yes, can you believe it? Anyway, he only had a few seconds to decide which painting to take. Of course, Vermeer's *The Concert* was the most valuable—and at just over two feet square, it also would have been one of the simplest to sneak out of the restaurant. But Rudy was worried that it would have been too easily missed. *Christ in the Storm on the Sea of Galilee* posed the same problem, and it was also much too large to smuggle out. He settled on *A Lady and Gentleman in Black*, thinking that it might not be missed as quickly. He rolled up the canvas, tucked it under his clothes, and sauntered out of the wine cellar with a multimillion-dollar heist of his own."

"Wasn't he worried the mob would trace the painting's disappearance back to him?" Amalia said.

"I asked him the same question. He said he figured the restaurant was such a busy location, with so many people coming in and out, that there would be an infinite number of people for the mob to suspect."

"Why didn't you report him to the police?" I inquired.

Laverne gave a long sigh, and her body sagged as if defeated.

"I should have done that, I know. But I felt a great deal of affection for Rudy. I didn't want to cause him any harm. And when he asked for my help in selling the painting, I'm ashamed to admit the thought of earning a fifty-percent commission on that sale blinded me from the truth—that I was simply aiding and abetting a criminal. Believe me, I've lived with that guilt ever since."

"Why did you think Walter Cobb would be interested in acquiring the painting?"

"I'd worked with him for a few years by that point, and I knew he was the sort of collector who liked to own things that were unique. He took a great deal of pleasure from knowing that no one else in the world possessed something he did. Ethically, I didn't know how he would feel about buying a stolen item—but he was the first person I thought of when Rudy asked for my help."

"And what was Cobb's reaction when you approached him with the idea?"

"He was hesitant at first, but I could tell it intrigued him. We had a series of conversations over the course of a few weeks. One thing that concerned him was how he would hide the painting so that no one knew he had it. Once he'd made up his mind, however, the deal came together pretty quickly."

"Did he share any details with you about how—or *where*—he planned to hide it?"

"No, I'm afraid not."

"Do you have any idea where that painting might be now?"

"I wish I could be more helpful. But really, that's all I know."

"Whatever happened to Aiken?"

Laverne's face became pale, and she was silent for several seconds. When she finally spoke, I had to lean in closer to hear her.

"I didn't hear from him after the sale. I assumed he'd moved far away, you know, to get away from the mob. But six months later, I saw his name and photo in the obituary section of the *Globe*.

"There was no mention of how he died. Yet, I can't help thinking those criminals figured out what he did and took their revenge. It chills me to the bone, imagining what they must have done to make him reveal who had the painting. For weeks afterwards, I would lie awake at night and listen for those monsters outside my door. When they didn't come for me, I figured maybe I was wrong and that Rudy died a peaceful death after all. But a part of me wonders if I owe him my life, because he was brave enough not to give up what he knew."

I took her hands in mine. "Ms. Pemberton, thank you for telling me the truth about what happened."

"So what happens to me now?"

"Not a thing. I made you a promise, and I intend to keep it. No one else has to know what you've told us. The statute of limitations on the sale of that stolen painting expired years ago, and nothing you've said today would help in recovering the other works. I'm sure those other items from the heist were moved again as soon as the mob realized the Rembrandt was missing."

"Thank you."

As Amalia and I stood up to leave, I paused and added: "I hope you find some peace after all these years."

Laverne leaned in close and whispered: "And I hope *you* keep your promise."

* * *

On our way out of the house, Amalia said: "That was quite a story."

131

"Yeah. I can see why she was reluctant to share it the first time."

Ms. Pemberton's account had filled in many gaps, and now I knew how Cobb had acquired his "treasure." But she was right to question how helpful her story would be to my case. I wasn't any closer to finding the actual painting than I was before.

However, I still had the realization I'd come to the day before, about the mention of Meredith in Cobb's journal perhaps referring to the *town* and not a person.

As we climbed into Amalia's jeep, I tossed her a proposition: "How would you like to take a road trip up to Meredith?"

Chapter 17

The drive up Route 93 from Andover, Massachusetts, to Meredith, New Hampshire, took about ninety minutes. By noon, Amalia was taking Exit 23 onto Route 104 East, and less than fifteen minutes later we were pulling into downtown Meredith.

We stopped for lunch at the Town Docks restaurant, where we had a beautiful view of Lake Winnipesaukee. Because the sun was shining and the weather was still warm, with the temperature hovering around sixty degrees, we ate outside at a picnic table right next to the water. Though slightly past their peak, the leaves still formed vivid splashes of goldenrod and mahogany red, and the sunlight danced on the surface of the azure water.

For the zillionth time, I marveled at how lucky I was to live in New England in the fall.

After lunch, we kept Amalia's jeep parked at the docks and walked to the town hall building, which was only a few streets away.

Inside the town hall, we were greeted by a female clerk sitting at a desk behind a pane of plexiglass. She had short brown hair and was wearing a white turtleneck sweater. The name plate on her desk read *Marcy Evans*.

"Hi, Marcy. My name is Parker Hanson, and I'm a private investigator from Manchester," I said, showing her my license. "I'm looking for someone who lives here in town and goes by the name of Beth or Elizabeth, but I don't have a last name. I'm wondering if you could give me the names and addresses of anyone who might fit this description?"

Marcy thought for a minute. "I could run a search of our property tax records and see what comes up. If they own land here in town, they should be listed in that database. But if they're just renting, then their name wouldn't appear in the search."

She typed on her computer keyboard, then disappeared behind a partition. A few seconds later, she emerged with a printed sheet of paper, which she handed over to me. The printout contained the names and addresses of six people named either Beth or Elizabeth.

I read through the names, but none of them were familiar to me.

There were a few chairs lined up along one wall of the town hall lobby. I sat down on one of the chairs, and Amalia sat next to me.

"Why don't you take the first three names on this list," I said to Amalia, "and I'll take the other three. See what you can learn about these women from a quick Internet search on your phone. We're looking for anything that might connect them with Walter Cobb in some way."

"Got it."

As Amalia and I conducted our search, Marcy's voice piped up from behind the plexiglass.

"You know, I couldn't help overhearing your conversation," she said. "Are you sure it's a *person* you're looking for?"

"What do you mean?" I replied.

"I don't know if you knew this or not, but there's also a *street* in Meredith named Beth Lane."

Amalia and I looked at each other in amazement, and I turned to Marcy with a wide grin. "Marcy, you're a godsend! Can we get a list of who owns property on that road?"

"Give me just a minute." Her fingers glided across the computer keyboard, and she emerged a moment later with another printout in her hand.

There were only five sets of names and addresses on this sheet of paper. One of the names instantly jumped out at me.

"Ty Wobblecart, sixteen Beth Lane." The hair on the back of my neck stood up as I read the name aloud, and I showed it to Amalia.

"What's so special about him?" she asked.

"Ty isn't a very common name. But it just so happens that one of the most famous Tys in history was a baseball player whose last name was 'Cobb.'"

"Like Walter Cobb!"

"Exactly. And not only that, but look at the letters in the last name. They form a perfect anagram of 'Walter Cobb.'"

"So you think it's a phony name?"

"It's got to be. What do you say we check out this address?"

* * *

Beth Lane was only a mile from the town hall building, so we decided to walk.

We continued up the hill from the town hall on Main Street, then turned right onto Water Street and right again onto Red Gate Lane. Half a mile up the road, Red Gate Lane curved sharply to the left, and we continued straight onto a dirt road called Bonney Shores Road.

The sun beamed down brightly from the topaz sky, and my reconstructed heart was racing as we turned onto Beth Lane from Bonney Shores Road after another half a mile of walking.

The lane looped down by Lake Waukewan, a small offshoot of Winnipesaukee. Number sixteen was only a tenth of a mile down the road on the left. There was no mailbox, and the driveway stretched for about a hundred yards and then disappeared around a bend to the left.

We made our way cautiously down the driveway. As we rounded the bend, the house came into view.

It was a modest, one-story Cape-style ranch bisected by a single large gable with an arch window. The house had shingle-style cedar siding with white trim and shutters. The property was right on the lake, with a neatly mowed backyard that sloped down to the water's edge. As Cobb had passed away about a month before, I assumed he used a landscaping business to cut the grass and that he'd prepaid for the season.

I knocked and rang the doorbell. There was no response.

I took out the Swiss Army knife I carried wherever I went, chose the hole-punch tool, and set to work picking the lock.

"You're going to break in?" Amalia asked. "What if we're wrong about this being Walter Cobb's house?"

"Then we'll have a pretty amusing story to tell the judge."

Within thirty seconds, I had the front door open, and Amalia and I slipped inside.

The first thing we saw was the stunning view of the lake.

We were standing inside a great room that was open to the peak of the gable, with exposed beams and a large stone fireplace in the center. The back wall of the house was made almost entirely of glass. Sunlight filled the room, and the calm waters of Lake Waukewan shimmered in the midafternoon sun.

To our left was a state-of-the-art kitchen and dining area. To our right were two bedrooms with a connecting bath in between.

Arranged in front of the fireplace were two red leather chairs and a sofa. The hearth contained a gas fireplace insert, and the chimney appeared to be purely decorative.

Although there were no open windows, the air inside the house smelled fresh.

"I expected it to smell musty in here," Amalia said.

"Cobb probably had an air exchange system installed," I said. "He was an architect before he become a full-time collector."

We searched the house for any sign of the painting, starting with the two bedrooms. While I combed through the closets, looking for hidden doors or compartments, Amalia checked under the beds, behind the headboards and dressers, and under the mattresses.

Finding nothing in the bedrooms, we moved through the rest of the house.

As I was examining the fireplace, I realized the surface actually consisted of artificial stone tiles that formed a realistic-looking veneer. And as I looked even more closely, I noticed a rectangular section of tiling about four and a half feet tall by three and a half feet wide was indented instead of being flush with the rest of the surface.

Those happened to be roughly the same dimensions of *A Lady and Gentleman in Black*, I realized.

"Amalia, come look at this!" I called out.

She joined me at the hearth and ran her fingers along the inset section of tiling.

"This could be a panel that slides behind the rest of the stone façade to reveal the painting!" she exclaimed, confirming my suspicion.

She tried sliding it and pressing on it, but neither action caused it to move.

"Do you see any mechanism that would open the panel?" I asked.

We looked for some kind of hidden switch or lever. Amalia tried the light switches on all the walls, but none of them triggered the panel. The only possible solution we found was a small, diamond-shaped hole in the stone façade, just above the mantel.

"This hole looks like it might be meant for a specially designed key," Amalia noted.

We scoured the house again, this time looking for a key that would fit into the hole. But our search came up empty.

"We could try to pry the panel open," Amalia suggested, indicating the decorative poker hanging next to the hearth.

"No, I don't think we should do that. The painting is too valuable. If it *is* behind that panel, I don't want to risk damaging it."

I sat down in one of the leather chairs facing the mantel and imagined a cozy fire flickering in the hearth before me. Beyond the fireplace, I could see the crystal-clear waters of Lake Waukewan glistening in the day's waning sunshine.

The house itself would be an ideal place to enjoy a stolen Rembrandt in solitude, I concluded—and the chairs in front of the fireplace would be the perfect vantage point from which to do so.

I was as sure as I knew the jersey numbers of the players on that season's Bruins roster that a priceless painting that had been missing for thirty-five years lay just a few feet away from where I was currently sitting, hidden behind a thin veneer of PVC painted to look like stone.

But for the moment, we had no way of getting to it safely.

Chapter 18

I spent Monday night tossing and turning in bed, my mind grappling with the question of where the key that operated that sliding panel might be hidden.

Key in C.

Corner lot, November 15.

Walter Cobb had written those words in his journal as a clue to the key's location.

But what did they mean?

By Tuesday morning, I was no closer to a solution. But I couldn't dwell on this question any longer. I had signed up to help paint the church that day, and I was hoping this activity might finally give me a chance to look inside Jonah Keefe's office for information about Project Abaddon.

When I arrived at the church at a quarter to ten, Pam and James Arsenault were already standing outside the side door, waiting to help paint. They were wearing clothes spattered with the evidence of similar labors from before.

Danny Coffey joined us a few minutes later, and at five minutes past ten, Charlie Dawes arrived. He unlocked the side door, and we all filed inside.

The church's side door was connected to an alarm system, and I pretended to look at my phone while I recorded Dawes as he disarmed the system. I figured I might need a backup plan if I wasn't able to find the information I was looking for during this volunteer session, and it would be helpful to know how to disable the alarm in case I had to break into the building.

As luck would have it, I was tasked with painting the hallway outside Keefe's office along with Coffey, while the Arsenaults worked with Dawes in the downstairs kitchen area. As I opened up a gallon of Behr Swiss Coffee semigloss paint, I realized it might have been purchased by Jonah Keefe on the same day I was following him at the Home Depot in Concord.

"I heard you wanted to be a professional wrestler?" I asked Coffey as we rolled out the paint on the walls.

Coffey grunted in response. "Not in the cards."

"Sorry it didn't work out. Did you get to meet any of the pros?"

"Uh-uh."

Not the best conversationalist.

We worked in silence for half an hour, until Pam Arsenault came up from the kitchen.

"Charlie and James would like your help in moving a few things," she told Coffey. "I thought we could switch places for a while."

Pam proved to be a lot chattier than Coffey. I wasn't sure how helpful her insight was to my investigation, but I learned there was no love lost between her and Livy Keefe.

"I'm not someone who usually speaks badly about another person, but that Livy Keefe really steams my greens," she said. "Last year, I made these crocheted mushroom sprites for our annual fundraiser, and they were a big hit. They're basically little mushrooms with eyes and feet, and everyone thought they were so cute. I made twice as many for this year's event, and when I show up, what is Livy selling? Crocheted tree fairies with eyes, mouths, and arms."

"That's not cool," I said. "What'd you do?"

"I told her: 'Livy, I don't appreciate you stealing my idea.' And do you know what she said to me? 'Well, Pam, you need to get over yourself. This fundraiser isn't about you, it's about making money for the church.'"

By noon, we were done painting the hallway—but I hadn't had a moment to myself all morning. I was frustrated that I hadn't had a chance to do any further digging around.

Pam and I joined the others in the downstairs kitchen area, and the five of us finished painting that space by twelve thirty.

"Are we painting Jonah's office, too?" I asked Charlie Dawes.

"Nah. I don't actually have a key to that office. Reverend Keefe is a really private guy."

Dawes thanked us for our help, and we called it a day.

Volunteering at the church hadn't turned out as I'd hoped, and I was quickly running out of time. The "final prep" for Project Abaddon was now only two days away, and I still had no idea what the plan entailed.

If I could just get access to Keefe's office, that might change quickly.

My shoulders ached from painting all morning, and my tee shirt was plastered to my torso. But the one good thing to come out of this effort was that I now knew how to disarm the church's alarm system.

It was time to put this new knowledge to use.

* * *

Twelve hours later, I was seated in Amalia's jeep. Amalia was driving, and we were on our way to the church. We were both dressed in black and wearing gloves. The clock on the jeep's dashboard read 12:54 a.m.

"I don't want to make a habit out of this," Amalia said, referring to breaking and entering for the second time in as many days.

"Desperate times, yadda yadda," I responded.

"Did you happen to notice if there are any cameras inside or outside the building?"

"Nothing obvious. I suppose there could be hidden cameras somewhere."

"Then we better be fast."

We parked a few blocks from the church and walked the rest of the way in the dark, a waxing crescent moon illuminating the empty streets around us. We were both carrying flashlights so that we could see inside the building without turning on any lights.

When we reached the church, I used my Swiss Army knife to pick the side door's lock, and we slipped inside. Turning on my flashlight, I aimed the beam at the security system console and typed in the number I'd seen Dawes use earlier that day.

For a moment, nothing happened—and I briefly panicked as I wondered if I'd gotten the code wrong. Then, the system's flashing lights turned off, and I breathed a quick sigh of relief.

In less than a minute, I'd picked the lock on the door to Keefe's office, and we began looking for information on Project Abaddon. While Amalia searched inside the filing cabinet, I rifled through the desk's drawers.

The bottom drawer held a collection of dark green hanging folders, each containing a copy of one of Keefe's sermons. The middle drawer was stuffed with blank lined notepads, envelopes, and church stationery. The top drawer contained an assortment of pens, pencils, paper clips, a stapler, and sticky note pads of various colors.

I was about the close the drawer when I noticed some writing on one of the sticky note pads. Training my flashlight on the pad, I saw a familiar word—and a series of letters and numbers that meant nothing to me. I pulled the sticky note off the top of the pad and put it in my pocket.

On top of Keefe's desk were some theology books and a desk calendar. As I was scanning the calendar, a particular entry caught my eye.

"Hey Mal, check this out—" I began.

As I was speaking, the door to Keefe's office shot open. Three figures loomed in the hallway outside, silhouetted by the moonlight streaming through a hall window.

Two of the figures were complete strangers to me. They towered in size over the third, whom I recognized as Danny Coffey.

Coffey was a big guy himself, about six feet tall and at least two hundred twenty-five pounds. But next to the others, he looked like a garden gnome. He was holding a tire iron, and a malevolent grin was etched on his face, as if he were looking forward to swinging the instrument against my head.

"Parker. What are you doing in this office?"

"Oh, is that where I am? I must have taken a wrong turn at the altar."

"You know you're breaking and entering, right?"

"So call the police. Here, I'll dial for you." I reached for the phone on Keefe's desk. "They might like to know about Project Abaddon, by the way."

"Actually, we thought we'd take care of the problem ourselves. Right, boys?"

As if in response, the two larger men stepped past Coffey

and entered the room.

"It's a good thing you wanna learn about our Holy Father," Coffey snarled. " 'Cuz now you're gonna meet him."

Chapter 19

As Thing One and Thing Two advanced on Amalia and me, I turned my flashlight on them and switched on the high power, aiming the light directly in their eyes. The two men blinked and stepped back, shielding their eyes with their hands. It was just the opening Amalia needed to get the upper hand.

She rushed forward and stepped down hard on the left knee of the guy to our left. I heard a sickening crunch, and he screamed in agony and dropped to the floor.

Almost simultaneously, she drove the heel of her right hand up into the face of the guy to our right, hitting him squarely in the nose. His head jerked back and he slumped against the filing cabinet, passed out cold.

Most people would have stood rooted to the spot, watching this action unfold. But Coffey had clearly been in his share of street fights before, because while this was going on, he sprang forward without hesitation and swung the tire iron at Amalia's head with tremendous force.

The steel rod barely missed her skull as she dodged to the left just in time, the blow glancing off her right shoulder instead.

Grunting in pain, Amalia stepped toward Coffey so that she was inside his swing radius and delivered a jab into his solar plexus with her left fist, causing him to drop the tire iron. Then she stepped back quickly so he couldn't grab her and wrestle her to the ground with his bulk.

Unfortunately, there wasn't a lot of room to maneuver in Keefe's office—and the goon who was writhing on the floor with a broken leg thrust out his arm, catching Amalia by the heel and sending her reeling.

Coffey saw his chance and leaped on top of her. He must have outweighed her by a hundred pounds, and despite her considerable skill, he managed to overpower her long enough to get her into a choke hold.

I grabbed the first heavy object I could find from Keefe's desk—an ivory paperweight in the shape of a crucifix—and brought it down on the back of Coffey's head, stunning him enough for Amalia to pry herself loose.

She unleashed a vicious elbow that caught Coffey in the middle of his forehead, and he crumpled at her feet, lying motionless.

Amalia dropped to her knees, breathing heavily.

"Should we call the police?" she asked.

"I see no reason to implicate ourselves in a crime."

The only one of the three hoodlums who was still conscious was the guy with the shattered knee.

"Do you have a cell phone?" I asked him.

When he nodded, I told him to call for an ambulance. Then I helped Amalia up, and we left the church.

* * *

As we walked back to Amalia's jeep, I asked her if she needed medical attention for her shoulder.

"No, it's just a bad bruise," she said, wincing. "I'm sorry we didn't find anything useful. I guess that was a flop."

"That's not exactly true."

"What do you mean?"

"Before those goons burst in, I got a good look at Jonah Keefe's desktop calendar. In the square for this Saturday the sixteenth, he had written the initials: *PA.*"

"Project Abaddon!"

"That's what I figure, too."

"So you think this Saturday is when the attack will occur?"

"I do. That doesn't give us a lot of time to—"

I noticed that Amalia's jaw was clenched, and the blood had rushed to her face.

"What's wrong?" I said. "I realize that's only a few days away, so we'll need to double our efforts if we're going to figure out where—and how—the attack will take place."

"I know *where* it will take place," Amalia said, so quietly that I had to strain my ears. "At least, I have a pretty good idea."

She had stopped walking, and as she looked up at me, I saw a glint of rage in her eyes.

"This Saturday is the LGBTQ+ History Month celebration in downtown Concord," she noted grimly.

My heart leaped into my throat. "The event Kris is involved in planning."

"That's right."

"*Shit.*"

It made perfect sense. What better target for a bunch of Christo-fascist thugs than a gay history celebration?

"We'll find a way to stop it," I said, putting my hands on her shoulders.

"You better believe it."

I suddenly remembered the sticky note in my pocket. I fished it out and handed it to Amalia. "I found this in one of the desk drawers as well. Any idea what it means?"

"*Trig - M249*," she read, and she looked up at me in shock.

"What is it?"

"An M249 is a type of weapon used in the U.S. military," she said.

"So this is probably the weapon the guy known as 'Trig' is gonna use for the attack?"

"I would guess so."

"What's wrong now?" Amalia's face had turned from crimson to bone white, the blood draining as quickly as it had appeared.

"You'd know if you were familiar with an M249."

"Tell me."

"It's a lightweight machine gun that fires a five-point-five-six millimeter cartridge. That's a bullet about an inch and a half long. It's intended for a range of up to eight hundred meters, which is half a mile. It supports a two-hundred-round magazine of linked ammunition, and a gunner can fire all two hundred rounds in about fifteen seconds."

"Good lord. If we don't stop the attack, the results will be..."

"Catastrophic," she finished.

Chapter 20

Amalia and I met Detective Connor for breakfast at the Red Arrow Diner on Loudon Road in Concord the next morning. He looked apologetic as he slid into the booth across from us.

"You're not gonna be happy," he began.

I'd called him earlier that morning and told him what we suspected, based on the information we'd obtained the night before. Connor had passed what I said along to Chief of Police Dalton Keane.

"Lemme guess. Your chief doesn't think the intel we have is solid enough to act on."

"I tried, Parker. I really did. But the chief has a point. There's nothing definitive here, just your own interpretation of a few highly ambiguous scribbles."

"What if we're right, though?" Amalia interjected. "We're talking about the potential for mass casualties."

"And if you're wrong? Then we've just wasted thousands of dollars for a wild goose chase. Even worse, we've diverted those resources from keeping the public safe from actual crimes."

"Shouldn't we err on the side of caution here?" I asked.

"And do what, exactly? Cancel the event? We can't do that

based on what little information we have suggesting an attack might occur. Our local businesses are counting on the extra money they stand to gain from the influx of visitors to the city that day. That could mean tens of thousands of dollars in additional revenue."

"What about asking the state police for more manpower?"

"We'll already have a strong police presence as it is. Without hard evidence, there's no way the state would approve further support on such short notice."

"This doesn't have anything to do with the chief being a member of the church, does it? For all we know, he could even be in on the plot."

Connor gave me a look like I'd just sneezed on his chateaubriand at a swanky restaurant.

"Watch it, Parker. I consider you a friend, but you're skating on thin ice with that remark."

* * *

Connor had a point. I didn't know the chief well enough to be tossing around accusations like that.

On the other hand, the idea that Chief Dalton Keane was somehow involved in Project Abaddon couldn't just be dismissed out of hand. In breaking up the gun smuggling ring just a few months earlier, I'd been embroiled in a case involving corrupt public officials. Who was to say it wasn't happening again?

Maybe Chief Keane wasn't part of the supposed plot. Maybe he was just prejudiced against the LGBTQ+ community.

Or maybe I just needed to do my job better. Maybe we needed more solid proof in order to convince him to take the threat seriously.

Whatever the reality, Amalia and I still had a lot of work to do. We needed to collect more information about the attack we suspected would happen in just a few days' time—and we needed it quickly.

When we left the diner, we drove back to Manchester and stopped at the Mall of New Hampshire, where Kris worked as a fashion specialist at Macy's, to talk with her about the LGBTQ+ History celebration she was helping to plan in Concord.

"Is there any chance you could just cancel it?" Amalia asked, recounting our conversation with Detective Connor.

"I don't want to do that," Kris said. "I know you're worried, and I appreciate that. But we have a lot riding on this event. It's taken us years to convince the city that celebrating LGBTQ+ history is important. Canceling now would undermine all that hard work. And besides, it's not just my call. It would have to be a full committee decision."

"Surely the committee deserves to know what we suspect might happen at the event?" I queried.

"You're right. I can try to convene an emergency meeting over Zoom tonight to discuss it. Would you be able to sit in and describe your theory?"

"Of course."

If the celebration was going to continue as planned, then we needed to know as many details about the event itself as we could learn, in order to anticipate how an attack might unfold—and also how to stop it.

"Tell me about LGBTQ+ History Month," I asked Kris. "I thought it was in June, not October?"

"You're thinking of Pride Month," she said.

"What's the difference?"

"Pride Month is a celebration of who we are and our right to exist, and it's held in June to commemorate the Stonewall uprising in 1969, widely considered to be the start of the gay rights movement. History Month highlights the past struggles and achievements of the LGBTQ+ community."

She continued: "In 1994, a high school history teacher in Missouri named Rodney Wilson was teaching his class about the Holocaust, and when he explained to his students that if he'd lived in Europe then, he probably would have been executed for being gay, he realized how little most of the public knows about LGBTQ+ history. He started LGBTQ+ History Month to help fix that. He decided to hold it in October because schools and colleges were in session then, but also to coincide with National Coming Out Day and the first march on Washington for gay rights back in 1979."

"What will the History Month celebration this Saturday in Concord involve?"

"The event will take place from one to four p.m. along North Main Street, between Loudon Road and Route 202. That entire five-block section will be blocked off from traffic, so people can walk safely up and down the street. We'll have booths set up along both sides of the road, with exhibits featuring important people and events from LGBTQ+ history in New Hampshire and nationwide."

"Like what?"

"Well, here in New Hampshire, the nineteen fifties saw the emergence of an LGBTQ+ community in Portsmouth— and the city's first gay bar, the Seacoast Club, opened in 1957. However, the LGBTQ+ community remained mostly underground until the seventies, when there was a rise in activism in the state.

"In the early 1970s, students at the University of New Hampshire founded the Gay Student Organization, but this group faced heavy opposition, including from the governor at the time, and the university pulled its support. The GSO sued, and the state Supreme Court ruled in the students' favor in 1974.

"New Hampshire law has protected people against discrimination based on their sexual orientation since 1998. In 2007, the state became the first in the country to pass a civil union law recognizing LGBTQ+ couples through legislative action instead of the courts. Two years later, New Hampshire passed a law allowing same-sex marriages. And in 2018, U.S. Representative Chris Pappas was elected as the state's first openly gay member of Congress. These are just some of the people and events that will be recognized on Saturday."

"Who's organizing the event?" I asked.

"The city of Concord is organizing it in partnership with New Hampshire Pride, of which I'm a member."

"What time will North Main Street be closed off to traffic, and when can people start setting up their exhibits?"

"Traffic will be closed off starting at noon, and vendors can set up their exhibits then."

* * *

Equipped with information about the LGBTQ+ History Month celebration in Concord and what it entailed, Amalia and I decided to return to Concord for a little reconnaissance work. We wanted to walk along North Main Street to see the site of the event firsthand, while trying to put ourselves in the shoes of someone who might be planning an attack.

We parked in a spot on North Main Street directly in front of the New Hampshire State House building and started walking south, toward Route 202.

Unlike Manchester, whose downtown boasts some of the

tallest buildings in northern New England—including the 274-foot-tall City Hall Plaza building, the tallest building north of Cambridge, Massachusetts—downtown Concord has no such towering structures. All the buildings along North Main Street were only three or four stories high.

But still plenty tall enough for a shooter to spray the street below with ammunition from one of the upper-floor windows.

Since our run-in with Danny Coffey and his goons the night before, I had been thinking about the identity of the "RA" mentioned in the Project Abaddon document. Not only was Robert Allen a fan of fast cars, but I'd also seen him talking with Coffey at the church this past Sunday.

Those two facts in combination led me to believe he was probably involved in the plot.

"Here's what we think we know," I said. "We think someone armed with an M249 plans to start shooting at the crowd during the event on Saturday. We think Jonah Keefe was in charge of securing access to one of the buildings here along Main Street as a vantage point for the shooter to use. And we think someone with the initials RA, whom I believe to be Robert Allen, may be positioned as a getaway driver for the shooter."

"If this street is blocked off to traffic, then the driver will have to be parked on one of the parallel roads running behind these buildings," Amalia noted. "We're probably looking for a building that has a rear exit opening out onto a back alley. If it were me, I'd choose a building on the east side of Main Street," she said, pointing to our left, "because then you'd be closer to Route 93 for an easier getaway."

"Makes sense."

We crossed the street and cased the buildings along that

stretch of the road, looking for facilities with rear exits and office spaces on the upper floors. As we compiled a list, we quickly realized there were many buildings that met these criteria: at least a few dozen, if we counted the ones on the other side of the street as well.

Recognizing that we weren't going to be able to narrow our focus by staying on our current course, we changed up our approach. We headed to the City Hall on Green Street and spent the rest of the afternoon tracking down the names and telephone numbers of the owners and/or managers of all the buildings with rear exits along that five-block segment of North Main Street.

Once we'd secured that information, we divided up the list and called each owner or building manager to ask if anyone named Jonah Keefe had rented space on an upper floor recently. According to the Project Abaddon document, the person in charge of building access in the purported plot was "JK," which we assumed stood for Jonah Keefe—so we figured Keefe might have contacted the owner or manager of one of the buildings to rent space from which to launch the attack.

Between the two of us, Amalia and I must have made more than twenty phone calls—but to no avail. Either Keefe had arranged access in some other way, perhaps through an intermediary who was already leasing building space on North Main Street, or else he'd used an assumed name when he made the arrangements.

Discouraged that we weren't able to pinpoint the actual building to be used in the suspected shooting, we headed back to Manchester.

* * *

Kris was able to get members of the steering committee

together for a seven thirty Zoom meeting to talk about the attack I feared was planned for the event on Saturday. Amalia was working at the Tipsy Moose during the Zoom call, but Kris sent me the meeting link so I could share our thoughts with the group.

After Kris introduced me, I told the committee members about the Project Abaddon document that P.J. Warner had found and the calendar entry and sticky note scrawl that seemed to confirm our suspicions about what it meant.

"So to recap," the committee chair said, "your only real evidence that a shooting might occur is an ambiguous document you discovered a few weeks ago and the initials 'PA' on a desktop calendar?"

"Well, yeah—that and several years of experience as a trained investigator."

"I agree that it's pretty thin," another member said. "But on the other hand, we're responsible for the safety of everyone that comes to the event. What if Mr. Hanson's instincts are correct? Should we really be taking that chance?"

"If we cancel the celebration on the basis of just a hunch, we'll never get back the trust of the city again," the chair noted.

After another few minutes of debate, the committee members voted on whether the event should continue as planned. The motion to go through with the celebration on Saturday carried, five to four—with Kris casting the deciding vote in favor.

I wondered how her vote would be received when Amalia found out.

* * *

With the LGBTQ+ History celebration set to continue, and the police not tightening security, it fell to Amalia and me to thwart the suspected plot. But we still didn't know who the shooter was—or where they were going to be positioned.

According to the Project Abaddon document that Warner had discovered, the "final prep" for the attack was scheduled for the next day. Amalia and I planned to follow Jonah Keefe and Robert Allen, whom we assumed were the "JK" and "RA" referred to in the document, for the entire day—sticking to them like gum sticks to a middle schooler's hair to see what we could find out.

It might be our last chance to learn something useful before the attack occurred.

Chapter 21

Jonah Keefe knew who I was, but he didn't know Amalia. Therefore, it made sense for Amalia to watch Keefe and for me to shadow Robert Allen on Thursday.

Amalia had taken the evening off from work, and Callie had agreed to sleep at my apartment so she could take care of Minerva for me. We were prepared to follow our quarry all night if that's what it took to observe their "final prep" activities.

Allen lived in an apartment complex in downtown Concord. By five thirty a.m., I was parked where I could see both Allen's Dodge Challenger and the front door to his apartment building. A thermos of ice water sat in the cup holder of my center console, and a cooler with two chicken salad sandwiches with honey crisp apple slices on ciabatta bread rested on the passenger's seat beside me.

At seven o'clock, a yellow van with the words "Bright Bulb Electricians" pulled up to the building's front entrance. Allen came out and hopped into the van's passenger seat, and the van drove off.

I followed the van to a residence in Bow. The van pulled into the driveway and I drove past, then turned around and parked a few hundred yards up the street.

Allen and the driver got out of the van. They grabbed some electrical equipment from the back of the vehicle and disappeared into the house.

I called up my nineties playlist, which had left off at Nirvana's haunting acoustic rendition of the David Bowie song "The Man Who Sold the World" from *MTV Unplugged*, and settled in for a long wait.

Shortly after ten thirty, Allen and his colleague emerged from the house, apparently finished with their job. They loaded the gear into the back of the van and drove away. I followed them as they returned to Concord, stopped for lunch at a McDonald's drive through, and continued on to another residence off Route 3 near the Boscawen line.

While Allen was inside the house, working on his second electrical job of the day, I texted Mal to see if her stakeout was any more interesting than mine.

Nothing to report, she wrote back. *All's quiet here as well.*

At three fifteen, Allen and his colleague finished their second job. The van brought Allen home.

Allen was inside his apartment building from three thirty to five thirty. When he came outside again, carrying a brown suede jacket, I saw that he had showered and changed into a long sleeved polo shirt and tan pants. He got into his car and drove to a local Applebee's.

I waited a few minutes, then entered the restaurant. Allen was sitting alone at the bar. I requested a table where I could watch him and ordered a salad and an unsweetened iced tea.

Allen ordered some kind of blue-tinted drink in a bowling-ball-sized goblet and a chicken quesadilla. He tried chatting up two women who sat next to him but failed to recognize their indifference. He didn't talk with anyone else at the bar, and when he finished his meal, he left.

I followed him back to his apartment. He entered the building around seven thirty.

I texted Mal again: *Any sign of Keefe?*

Her reply was brief: *No.*

I waited and watched for another six hours, but Allen never reemerged. At one thirty a.m., exhausted, I set my alarm for five thirty and caught a few hours of sleep.

* * *

When I woke up, it was still dark outside. I checked my email and fired off a text to Callie, thanking her for taking care of Minerva and updating her on what was happening.

At six o'clock, as the sky began to brighten toward the east, I called Amalia. "Are you still outside Keefe's house?"

"Yes. He didn't go out at all last night."

"Neither did Allen. Maybe the 'final prep' referred to in that document happened over the phone or online."

"That was my thought as well. Or maybe they canceled it out of precaution. What do you want to do?"

"Can you stay on Keefe again today? Let's give it until this afternoon to see if anything happens."

"Got it."

I watched the sun peek over the horizon, an orange ball of fire slowly advancing. Under any other circumstances, I would have marveled at the natural beauty unfolding before me.

But in that moment, all I felt was looming desperation. We hadn't learned anything new the night before, and we were running out of time. With every passing hour, it seemed like that giant ball of fire in the sky was closing in on me personally, on the verge of consuming me in a scorching conflagration.

I followed Allen around town for a second straight day. Once again, he led me to a series of job sites and no more.

As late afternoon encroached, and it was obvious the stake-out wasn't getting us anywhere, I called Amalia. "Any luck?"

"Nothing."

The clock on my car's dashboard read 4:10 p.m. Although it was digital, I could swear I heard a ticking sound, counting the seconds elapsing as the festival approached.

Less than twenty-four hours away, and getting closer every minute.

Yet, we still weren't any closer to averting what could be a tragedy on a massive scale.

"Thanks, Mal. I'm calling it."

"Roger that."

I sat in my car as the shadows lengthened, my anguish almost palpable.

Though I knew in my head that it didn't make sense to feel this way, in my heart I believed I was personally responsible for the safety of every person taking part in Concord's celebration of LGBTQ+ history the next day.

And after two full weeks of investigating, we still lacked the critical piece of information we needed to prevent an attack.

Who was the shooter?

Amalia and I could continue shadowing Jonah Keefe and Robert Allen throughout the next day's event. But there was no indication that either man knew how to use an M249 or would be directly involved in the attack itself. Following them around wasn't guaranteed to lead us to the actual perp.

If the person referred to as "Trig" in the Project Abaddon document was indeed responsible for procuring the weapon, then it stood to reason he was also the best candidate for *using* it. And I had no clue who this person was—or how to stop him.

I was almost out of ideas.

Except for one.

It was a long shot. Kind of like pulling the goalie with five minutes left in the third period of a playoff elimination game in hockey when you're down by two or more goals.

But it was the only option I could think of.

Detective Connor had mentioned that Todd Primo controlled the gun trafficking trade in the state. Maybe Primo knew who'd been looking to acquire an M249 recently.

With mere hours left before what I feared would be a horrific attack, I was so desperate that I was willing to consider the unthinkable.

I was going to ask a mob boss for help in preventing a crime.

Chapter 22

I took Primo's business card from my wallet, holding it by the tip of the corner like it was covered in deadly toxins, and dialed the number embossed in gold.

Primo's voice boomed from my phone's speaker.

"Parker! Have you come to your senses at last?"

Actually, just the opposite. This phone call was evidence that I was losing my mind.

Primo knew my number from memory, or else he'd programmed it into his phone. In either case, he'd been waiting for me to call.

"Not over the phone," I said. "Let's meet in person. The first floor study room of the Concord Public Library in half an hour."

I wanted a quiet spot where we could talk without being overheard, but also someplace that was highly public so that I would feel secure. The first floor study room at the Concord Library was the perfect location. It had a door that we could shut, keeping our conversation private. Yet the door had a glass window pane, so we'd be visible to other people the whole time.

"What, do you have an overdue copy of *Wuthering Heights* or something?" Primo said.

"No. And if we're talking about the Brontë sisters, I always preferred *Jane Eyre*."

* * *

I asked Amalia to accompany me in case my meeting with Primo took a turn for the worse. She found what I was about to do highly amusing.

"If you've got a better idea," I told her, "I'm all ears."

Located on Green Street, behind the New Hampshire Legislative Office Building, the main branch of the Concord Public Library is a horizontal, two-story granite structure built in 1940. Its primary entrance is framed by a twenty-foot-tall glass window whose panes are crisscrossed diagonally by bronze muntins.

There were no parking spaces available in front of the library, so we turned right onto Prince Street and parked along this side street. I had called ahead to reserve the study room, and it was unoccupied when we arrived.

Primo kept us waiting inside the library for ten minutes before he showed up. Probably as a display of power, to remind me who was really in charge of the meeting.

He arrived with Nick the Neck trailing closely behind. Primo was wearing a forest green polo shirt, pleated khaki pants, and black lace-up shoes. Nick the Neck wore a shark-colored suit, again without a tie.

Nick broke off to browse through the graphic novel collection next to the study room, and Amalia moved to join him.

Maybe they would compare notes on their weapons of choice, I thought? Or pass the time by swapping amusing bodyguard stories?

Meanwhile, Primo sat across from me at the study room's conference table. He looked at me expectantly, waiting for me to begin.

I wasn't really sure how to start the conversation.

What do you say to a crime boss when you're politely declining his offer of employment—but you're also looking for his help on a separate case? Hallmark didn't make a card for that occasion.

Whenever I didn't know what to say, I always resorted to juvenile humor.

"This guy walks into a library and says to the woman behind the desk, 'I'll have a grilled cheese sandwich and a Coke.' The woman frowns at him and says, 'Sir, this is a *library*.' 'Oh, I'm so sorry,' he replies, and then he *whispers*: 'I'll have a grilled cheese sandwich and a Coke.'"

Primo sat silently for a few seconds, and then he chuckled.

"That's a good one. I like that. I like *you*, Parker. But I take it you're going to disappoint me?"

"Why do you say that?"

"Because I can read people. You don't reach a position like mine without having that skill. Do you know how many people I have to worry about on a daily basis? People coming for my job. Average Joes looking for revenge. Highly trained assassins aiming to take me out. I've learned to spot the telltale signs of trouble. Like the fear in a man's eyes when he's about to deny my request."

"*Touché*. Remind me never to play cards with you."

"But you didn't invite me here just to tell me this in person. A phone call or text message would have been so much easier, while also avoiding a confrontation. What else do you want to say to me?"

"Actually, you're half right. I *do* want something else from you. But even if I didn't, I still would have given you the courtesy of telling you face to face why I can't hand over that painting to you if I find it. I made a promise to my existing client, and I always keep my promises. It's a matter of personal integrity, not to mention my professional reputation. As a businessman, I hope you can appreciate that."

Primo sat back in his chair and stroked his chin, considering me for a moment. When he spoke again, it was in measured tones.

"You won't do what I asked, and yet you want something from *me*. Why should I even listen to what you have to say?"

I took a deep breath and dove in.

"I believe there's going to be a shooting tomorrow in downtown Concord, with the potential for mass casualties. I'm trying to prevent this from happening. But to do so, I need an important piece of information—something I think you possess. If you help me, you'll be saving countless lives. And if appealing to your innate sense of humanity isn't enough, helping me also makes smart business sense. In the aftermath of an event like that, the police are going to be extra vigilant, and it might be harder to operate for a while. What's more, the organization I suspect is behind the attack is a powerful church here in Concord that has crusaded against organized crime. If their leader goes down for planning the assault, you stand to benefit."

Again, Primo remained silent.

Finally, he leaned forward and said: "While you present a compelling case, it could also be argued that the police will be so distracted by the event you've described that we'll have *more* room to operate, at least in the short term. Still, I'd like to help you, Parker. I really would. But I never give up anything without getting something of significant value back in return. What you've described isn't enough. What else can you do for me?"

I was afraid it would come to this. But I was prepared for what Primo had to say.

"I have information about an FBI sting targeting your operation. How about an even trade—your intel for mine?"

"Now you've got my attention," he replied.

* * *

On the drive back to Manchester, I thought about what I'd just done.

I had made a deal with the Devil. Did it matter that my own Faustian bargain was struck not for my own personal gain, but for the benefit of others?

I had tipped off a mob boss about an FBI maneuver that could result in his arrest. I'd begun the conversation with a speech about personal integrity, and by the end, I was aiding and abetting a known criminal.

So, what did that make *me*?

Were my actions morally defensible? I was trying to prevent what I believed would be a mass tragedy. If it worked out as planned, would the ends justify the means?

After I'd advised Primo not to buy those diamonds from the South African courier because it was a sting operation, he told me he didn't know the identity of the person who'd sought to acquire an M249 machine gun offhand—but he could deliver it to me by the end of the night. He told me to watch for a text message from him later that evening.

Could I trust Primo to keep his word? I didn't have much choice in the matter. I hoped I wasn't being naïve.

"Penny for your thoughts?" Amalia said.

"You'd be overpaying."

"But you got what you wanted from the meeting with

Primo?"

"I think so. I just hope it was worth what I had to give up."

I didn't tell Amalia the price I'd paid for the information. To her credit, she didn't ask. All she said in response was, "The value of even one human life is immeasurable."

She had a point. But all I could think was: *Tell that to an actuary.*

* * *

Alone again in my apartment, I spent several anxious hours checking my phone repeatedly.

Callie joined me when her dance classes were over, though I'd warned her that I wouldn't be much company.

"So, like any other Friday night, then?" she cracked.

We spent the evening watching an old Marx Brothers film, but I think I paid more attention to my phone's screen than I did to the TV screen. Every time I heard my phone make a sound, I nearly leaped off the couch in anticipation.

Just after eleven p.m., my phone chimed again, signaling a new text message. This one was from Todd Primo, and it contained the two brief words I'd been waiting for all evening:

Will Tucker

Success!

I didn't know much about Tucker. I'd been introduced to him briefly after one of the church services I'd attended, but we hadn't exchanged any words aside from a polite greeting. From what I remembered, he mostly seemed to keep to himself.

I immediately called Detective Connor with the news.

When Connor answered the phone, he sounded groggy, as if he'd been asleep. "This better be good," he said.

169

"I think I know the identity of the shooter. His name is Will Tucker." I gave Connor Tucker's address from the church directory.

"Okay, looks like we're in business," Connor said, perking up. "I'll see if I can get a warrant to search Tucker's house for the illegal weapon."

When I hung up, Callie gave me a jubilant hug. I squeezed her tightly in response, then hung on for a few extra seconds.

"What's wrong?" she said, sensing that something was amiss.

"I don't know. I guess I'm just anxious about tomorrow. We think we know who the shooter is, but we still have to stop him."

Technically, that was true. But there was more to what I was feeling that I wasn't telling her.

Hearing Connor's voice on the phone was like absorbing a hard jab to the solar plexus.

Yes, we finally had the crucial piece of information I'd been trying to glean for a few weeks now.

But Connor had told me about that sting operation against Primo in confidence. And I'd gone and used it to help a dangerous felon escape justice.

I couldn't help thinking that if I'd just done my job more effectively, I wouldn't have had to undermine an important police action.

And I wouldn't have had to betray Connor's trust.

IV

To Catch a Keefe

Chapter 23

"I hope you're right about this," Connor huffed.

It was shortly after noon on Saturday, and we were racing along North Main Street in Concord—Amalia, Minerva, Connor, and I—trying to find Will Tucker before a mass shooting erupted.

At least, that's what I feared might happen at any minute.

Connor was referring to my theory that Tucker was perched near a window on the upper floor of one of the street's buildings as we spoke, an M249 at his shoulder, getting ready to fire into the crowd of people gathering for the city's LGBTQ+ History celebration that afternoon. He wasn't happy about spending his day off in support of Mal and me as we chased our suspicions about a massacre that might—or might not—actually be planned.

I thought about the implications of my assumption. What if we were right, but we were unable to stop the attack in time?

"I hope I'm *wrong*," I shot back.

* * *

When the police showed up to Tucker's apartment late on Friday night, he wasn't there. Neither was the M249. However, his blue Jeep Wrangler was still parked in the building's lot, undisturbed.

Connor had called me on Saturday morning with this update. He told me they'd stationed an unmarked car with two plainclothes detectives outside Tucker's building to watch for him in case he returned. He said the Concord PD also had requested air support from a state police helicopter to make sure no one was positioned on the rooftops of the buildings along North Main Street that afternoon.

If I was right about Tucker being the shooter, my guess was that he'd moved the machine gun into whatever upper-floor office space he was using for the attack earlier in the week. Maybe *he* was already in place as well, having slept in that space to ensure there would be no complications on the day of the shooting.

I'd thanked Connor for the update and hung up, then got out of bed and got dressed to take Minerva for a walk. It was only then that I'd had the brilliant, if rather obvious, inspiration to use Minerva to help us locate Tucker. As a purebred bloodhound, she was capable of following trails that were days old across busy streets and sidewalks, even in bad weather.

I called Connor back and told him my plan. Connor agreed to meet me in downtown Concord later that morning. I also called Amalia and enlisted her help.

Amalia and I drove to Tucker's apartment building with Minerva on a leash. I talked to the plainclothes detectives, and one of them let me into Tucker's apartment so that Minerva could learn the scent she would be tracking.

I let Minerva sniff around Tucker's bedroom and also took one of his tee shirts as a reminder. Then we'd met Connor in front of the New Hampshire State House building just before noon.

* * *

Minerva led us down North Main Street's eastern sidewalk toward Route 202, pausing occasionally to examine—and then reject—new smells as she tried to pick up Tucker's scent.

"I'm going to check the alleys behind these buildings for Robert Allen and his getaway vehicle," Connor said, branching off from our group.

"Good idea. Call me if you see anything."

With Minerva guiding us, Amalia and I wove our way through the throngs of people convening on North Main Street.

Even though the event itself wasn't scheduled to begin for another half hour, already the sidewalks were filling up. People were carrying boxes, lugging tables, and setting up exhibits on either side of the street. Early arrivers for the LGBTQ+ History celebration were milling around, pointing and chatting and laughing as they waited for the event to begin. And the usual downtown diners and shoppers were popping in and out of local establishments, pausing to gawk at the commotion around them.

I'd underestimated how hard it would be to fight the crowds that flooded North Main Street that afternoon. It was making me nervous that we wouldn't find Tucker in time.

"Is Kris here?" I asked Mal.

She didn't look pleased. "Yes. I tried to convince her to stay away. But she wasn't having it."

"Like a captain not leaving her ship."

"Aye, matey."

We reached the point where Main Street and Route 202 converged, and Minerva hadn't found Tucker's trail yet. We crossed the street and started working our way north again on the other side of the road.

I glanced at the clock on my phone. *12:42.* The celebration was officially scheduled to begin in less than twenty minutes.

While my eyes were locked on Minerva as she sniffed the ground at our feet, Amalia scanned the top floors of the buildings that surrounded us.

"There are a lot of open windows," she said. "No way to tell which one Tucker might be lurking behind."

"Of course it had to be unseasonably warm today."

Though Minerva was a squall of activity, moving from side to side amid the people cramming the sidewalk, our pace was slow and deliberate as we edged our way back up the street. I knew there was nothing I could do to speed up the process, but every minute that went by was like another twist of the handle on the vise encircling my chest.

"She *will* pick up the scent if it's here, right?" Amalia asked, a hint of desperation in her voice.

"Yes. I have complete faith in her." I had witnessed Minerva's uncanny tracking ability firsthand when I was on the other end of it nearly four months earlier, being hunted in the woods by the madman who'd owned her before. "This is going to work."

But while I spoke those words aloud, doubt was tunneling into my stomach like a colony of termites chewing a hole in a ceiling's main support beam.

We reached the block with the New Hampshire State House building, which was set back quite a bit from the road. Unless Tucker had found a way to conceal himself within this highly secure government building—while somehow sneaking a military-grade machine gun past a metal detector in the process—there were no more structures he could be shooting from.

"Oh, *shit*," Amalia said. "What if Tucker *entered* the building from the rear as well, and he never actually set foot on these sidewalks?"

My stomach folded in on itself, and the ground seemed to tilt beneath me.

It was already 1:09 p.m., and I realized that we had to repeat the same circuit we'd just completed—while this time having Minerva sniff around the back entrances to each building.

Before I could reply, a loud *BANG!* sent use diving for cover … until I realized it was just a display table that had been knocked over by mistake. Feeling embarrassed, we stood up and dusted ourselves off.

"Let's go," I said tensely. "Time's a-wasting."

Threading our way through the crowd, we crossed to the eastern side of the street again. We took Minerva through a side alley and around to the back of the buildings.

The tightening in my chest intensified as I realized it was now one fifteen. If I were planning the attack, I would have chosen to carry it out somewhere between 1:20 and 1:30 for maximum damage: Far enough beyond the official starting time for late arrivers to have joined the celebration, but not so far that people had begun to leave.

I didn't share what I was thinking with Amalia. But from the look on her face, I didn't have to—she was probably thinking the same thing.

The break in the clouds casting a pall over our situation was that, as we made our way south behind the buildings, we no longer had to deal with the hordes of people—and we were able to progress more quickly.

As we approached the ninth or tenth building we'd encountered with a rear entrance, Minerva began to spin in a circle.

Her tail wagged uncontrollably, and she reared her head back and bayed.

I knew that sound well. She'd picked up Tucker's trail.

If I'd launched myself off the ground at that moment, I'm pretty sure I would have floated away.

"Thatta girl," I said, wrapping the dog in a warm embrace.

* * *

Amalia and I crept behind Minerva as she led us up the stairs to the building's third floor. Mal had brought her Beretta nine-millimeter pistol, and she had her weapon drawn as we advanced.

There was a door at the end of the stairway, and it was locked.

I had texted Detective Connor to let him know we'd found Tucker's location. *Wait for backup*, he'd replied.

Given the urgency of the situation, though, we didn't want to risk any further delay.

The building was at least fifty feet deep from front to back. With all the noise from North Main Street, I figured that even if the third floor was one giant, open room, there was no way Tucker would hear me picking the lock.

I tied Minerva's leash to the stairway banister to keep her out of harm's way and told her to stay. Then I took out my Swiss Army knife and set to work on the lock.

Thirty seconds later, the door sprung open.

A long hallway stretched out before us and disappeared around a corner to the left. I could hear the ruckus from the street below.

We tiptoed down the hall, Amalia in the lead, and inched around the corner.

We found ourselves in a large office space at the front of the building. There were double pedestal metal desks with wooden writing surfaces scattered throughout the room. I noticed a sleeping bag and pillow on the floor in one corner— and an empty cello case beside it.

Tucker had positioned one of the desks beneath the windows looking down onto the street. One of these windows was wide open, and he had rested the automatic rifle's bipod legs on top of the desk, the weapon pointing down through the open window. His back toward us, he appeared to be adjusting the angle of the rifle to get a good shot.

His left hand was cradling the barrel, and his right hand was on the stock.

"Don't move!" Amalia shouted. She had her pistol aimed straight at Tucker's head. "You go for that trigger, I put a bullet in your brain."

My eyes were fixed on Tucker's right hand, and I held my breath. Time seemed to stop as I waited to see if his finger moved toward the trigger.

"Don't do it, asshole," Amalia hissed. "I've taken out enemies a lot more skilled than you."

My heart was running a marathon in my chest. But Amalia seemed cool and collected, her hand never wavering, as Tucker considered his options.

Slowly, he let go of the stock and extended his right arm out, palm facing up. Setting down the barrel of the gun, he did the same with his left arm.

Only then was I able to exhale.

Chapter 24

M y pulse rate hadn't yet returned to normal when I found myself seated in a conference room at the Concord Police Station along with Amalia, Detective Connor, and Chief Keane later that afternoon.

Connor had just recounted the day's events for his superior. Keane was silent for several seconds as he processed the information.

When he finally spoke, he sounded contrite.

"Parker, I owe you an apology. You were right about the attack. That was nice work by all of you today."

"Thanks, Chief."

"I fear I may have been blinded by my loyalty to the church. But the important thing is, we were able to avert a tragedy today—thanks to your persistence."

"Is Tucker talking?"

"No. He's lawyered up. Look like he'll be uncooperative."

"And what about Robert Allen?" Amalia asked.

"We picked him up on Low Avenue, behind the building where you found Tucker," Connor said. "He was parked in a white Toyota Camry that turned out to have stolen plates. But he's not talking, either. Says he knew Tucker from the church but had no idea about any shooting."

"He's lying," I said.

"Of course he is. But we have no proof. Not unless the two men implicate each other."

"And Jonah Keefe?"

"We sent a squad car to his house this afternoon," Keane said. "He was at home working in his yard. But his wife insists he was there all day, and the neighbors back her story. He expressed shock at the news about Tucker and denied any knowledge of the plot."

"Do you believe him?"

"Doesn't matter what I think," Keane declared. "Only what we can prove."

"But do you *believe* him?"

Keane sighed. "Let's put it this way. I won't be attending services at the Kingdom of Light church tomorrow morning— or ever again."

* * *

Callie spent Saturday night at my apartment. We made fresh pasta—ravioli filled with smoked salmon and ricotta cheese— and watched a screwball comedy with Cary Grant and Irene Dunne from the 1940s.

On Sunday morning, Callie headed to Durham to visit with her mother, while I got ready for church.

I was curious to learn how Keefe would handle the attempted shooting and what he might say about it—if anything—during the service. I also wanted to confront him face to face in the aftermath of the event.

I didn't have the energy to socialize before the service began, so I timed my arrival right at ten o'clock. I slipped into the church and sat in the back row just as the organist was finishing the prelude.

Livy's announcements contained no mention of what happened the day before. But Jonah alluded to it before launching into his sermon.

"I'd like to begin my remarks this morning by acknowledging a terrible incident," he said. "Yesterday afternoon in downtown Concord, one of our members was arrested when he was discovered with a military-style machine gun in his possession. The police allege he was planning to commit a mass shooting during the gay and lesbian history celebration that took place in our city."

As gasps and murmurs spread throughout the sanctuary, Keefe continued: "You all know how I feel about homosexuality. I believe it's a sin in God's eyes. That isn't just me talking, it's God's own word. Leviticus 18 tells us: *You shall not lie with a male as with a woman; it is an abomination*. But regardless of what I believe, I was shocked and saddened to hear that a member of our congregation would commit such an act. God does not want *us* to play God. He wants us to live our lives according to His word. Those who fail to do so will face His judgment in the afterlife."

Pointing to me in the back row, he added: "I understand that the newest member of our community, Parker Hanson, was instrumental in preventing the shooting from occurring. Let's all give him a round of applause for his heroism."

As the parishioners turned and clapped, I smiled through clenched teeth. Inside, I was stewing.

What a disingenuous asshole. Keefe was gloating, rubbing my nose in the fact that I couldn't connect him to the plot.

Immediately after the service, I made a beeline for the front of the sanctuary, squeezing my way through the throng of parishioners who were headed downstairs for coffee hour.

Keefe was collecting his written remarks from the altar. He saw me approaching and said, "Livy, darling, why don't you go downstairs—and I'll be down in a bit."

When she was out of earshot, I asked Keefe: "How long were you planning Project Abaddon? Was it months in the making, or did the whole thing come together fairly quickly?"

Keefe looked amused, like he was enjoying our repartee. "I have no idea what you're talking about," he smirked.

"Aren't you worried about Judgment Day? How are you going to explain to your God that you thumbed your nose at multiple commandments? *Thou shalt not lie. Thou shalt not kill.* How will you square your hypocrisy with your Creator? Or, do you not actually believe the words you're preaching?"

Keefe used his index finger to push his spectacles farther up the bridge of his nose, and he broke into a sanctimonious grin.

"I'm not worried about God's judgment. He knows I exist to do His bidding. If anyone should be worried, it's you. Who do *you* live to serve?"

* * *

I stormed out of the church, my fists clenched so tight that my hands felt numb, the anger pooling under my skin like molten lead.

I drove home slowly and deliberately, trying to calm my nerves. When I arrived home, I took Minerva for a walk around the block. Then I filled a water bottle and changed into nylon pants and hiking boots.

I got back into my car and drove for an hour to the Wapack Trail head in Greenfield. I hiked the Wapack Trail south for about two miles to the summit of North Pack Monadnock, then continued along the Cliff Trail for another two tenths of a mile. At the spot where the Cliff Trail merged with Ted's

Trail, there was a picturesque lookout to the east. I stopped at this lookout, found a perch on the exposed rock face, and gulped down some water while I gazed at the view and lost myself in thought.

It was bad enough that I hadn't been able to nab Governor Gordon in the gun smuggling scheme a few months before. There was no way I was going to let the same thing happen again with Jonah Keefe.

Whatever it took, I had to find a way to make sure justice was served in this case.

I needed the aid of someone within Keefe's circle of trust to help me catch him. And as I watched a red-tailed hawk gliding along a thermal current above me, I realized that I knew just such a person.

Even better, he owed me a favor. After all, I'd just saved his life one week earlier.

Chapter 25

Detective Connor and I met with Trace Gladstone in his trailer on Monday morning to discuss the plan. "You want my help with an undercover sting operation?" he asked, scurrying around the trailer and tossing empty beer cans into a plastic trash bag. He seemed embarrassed by the mess in his home, but genuinely touched that we would recruit his assistance—and an animated spirit that hadn't been there when I'd seen Gladstone in the hospital nine days earlier lit up his features.

"Yes," Connor said. "We believe Jonah Keefe was involved in planning a mass shooting in Concord this past Saturday. Luckily, we were able to foil the attack, and the suspected shooter is in custody. But he isn't talking, and we have no way of connecting Keefe to the plot at this point."

"The shooting targeted an LGBTQ+ event, and we believe it was ideologically motivated," I picked up. "We thought you could reach out to Keefe, posing as a sympathizer to the cause and trying to get him to take you into his confidence."

Gladstone didn't hesitate in responding. "Count me in," he said, a touch of pride in his voice—and I realized how powerful it must have been for him to feel needed, to apply his considerable skills once again to a covert operation.

We spent the next half hour discussing how the initial contact should unfold and what Gladstone should say. This conversation would be critical in establishing Keefe's trust. It had to be believable, while not scaring him off or arousing his suspicion.

We developed a rough script, and when Gladstone was ready, he dialed Keefe's number and put his phone on speaker mode so we could hear the conversation.

"Hello, Reverend Keefe? This is Trace Gladstone," he began, somewhat haltingly.

"Trace, it's good to hear from you," Keefe said. "How are you doing? Have you reconsidered my offer to come to our Sunday services?"

"I'm okay. I heard about what happened on Saturday when a member of the church was arrested, and I wanted to let you know that I'm sorry."

"Oh, yeah?" Keefe queried, unsure of where the conversation was going. "How so?"

"I'm sorry that he wasn't successful," Gladstone expounded, becoming more comfortable as he settled into his role. "Fucking queers are taking over everything." Gladstone was ad-libbing now, and I could see Connor visibly holding his breath. "Anyway, I wasn't sure if you had any knowledge of the plan, but if you did and you'd like to try it again, I'd be interested in participating. With my background, I think I could be useful to you."

Keefe was silent for a moment, and I worried that he saw through the ruse.

"Can you come to the church tomorrow night?" he said at last. "There's some people I'd like you to meet."

Gladstone looked over at Connor, who nodded. "Yes, I can

be there. What time?"

"Seven o'clock. We'll see you then."

* * *

With the hook set, all that remained now was to reel Keefe in.

I spent the rest of Monday and much of Tuesday either hanging out with Callie or volunteering for Hartman's campaign. At six thirty on Tuesday evening, Connor and I were stationed in the back of an unmarked police van parked around the corner from the Kingdom of Light Church. Six police officers dressed in tactical gear were waiting in the back of a panel truck parked across the street from our van.

Gladstone was inside our van as well, and a police technician was pinning a custom-made Alcoholics Anonymous recovery pin on the front of his sweatshirt. The pin had been outfitted with a miniature, high-tech camera and microphone to record both audio and video from his encounter with Keefe.

"Nice touch," Gladstone said, nodding toward the pin.

"Thanks," Connor said. "We figured Keefe wouldn't question why you were wearing an AA pin, even if he suspected a sting."

Connor was sitting in front of a laptop equipped to record the sound and images picked up by the surveillance device. He spent the next several minutes dispensing last-minute advice, though Gladstone didn't seem to need it.

As seven o'clock rolled around, he asked Gladstone: "You feel okay?"

"Let's do this," the ex-SEAL responded.

* * *

I watched over Connor's shoulder as Gladstone approached the church's front entrance, the ornate wooden doors growing in size on Connor's laptop screen.

Jonah Keefe met him inside the church vestibule. "Hello, Trace. It's good to see you. You're not wearing a wire, are you?"

"Fuck no," Gladstone said. The image from the camera momentarily went dark, and I assumed he was lifting up his sweatshirt to show Keefe his chest was bare.

Keefe smiled awkwardly. "I'm sure you can understand why I would ask. Why don't you follow me downstairs, and I'll introduce you to the others."

Keefe escorted Gladstone down to the coffee area, where Robert Allen and Danny Coffey were sitting at a table. Coffey had a purple bruise where Amalia's elbow had connected with his forehead one week earlier.

"I thought Allen was in jail?" I said to Connor.

"All we had on him was driving a car with a stolen license plate. He was out on bail the same day."

Keefe introduced Gladstone to the co-conspirators. Gladstone made sure he got a perfect image of each man's face as he shook their hands.

"Trace is a former Navy SEAL," Keefe told the others. "His skills could come in quite handy for us."

"So all of you were working with Will Tucker when he was arrested last weekend?" Gladstone asked.

"Yes," Keefe said. "But tell us, Trace, why are you interested?"

"There!" I exclaimed. "Keefe just admitted they were involved in the shooting plot."

"No," Connor corrected. "He said they were working with Tucker. But he didn't specify the context. We still need more."

I had talked over Gladstone's response, and so I only caught the tail end. "...Stupid queers deserve to die," he was saying.

Even though I knew Gladstone was playing a role—or at

least, I *hoped* he was acting—the words hit my ears like a slap upside the head.

Keefe leered at Gladstone's words, and my stomach felt queasy.

"Well," he told Gladstone, "we'd love to have you aboard."

"Before I say yes," Trace replied, "tell me what went wrong with the plan you had. Why didn't it work?"

"Some private dick got in the way," Coffey said.

"But you don't have to worry about him now," Keefe added. "He's being taken care of as we speak."

"Was there a leak in your operation? How did he know about the plan?"

"I'm afraid that was my fault," Keefe said. "I was careless with some notes I'd made, and I left them on a shared computer. But that won't happen again."

"Are you thinking you want to try another mass shooting? Or a different type of attack this time?"

"That's what we're hoping *you* can help us decide."

"I've heard enough." Connor spoke into his radio, addressing the officers in tactical gear: "Let's move in."

* * *

Ninety seconds later, the sound of boots clomping down stairs thundered through Connor's laptop, and I heard someone yell, "*Police! Stay where you are!*"

I watched as the tactical unit stormed into the picture and handcuffed Keefe, Allen, and Coffey without incident, then led them upstairs.

Connor and I got out of the van and met the group as they were exiting the church.

Gladstone came out first, and Connor slapped him on the back. "Nice work," he said.

"Yeah, thanks for your help," I told him. "We couldn't have done it without you."

"Felt like old times," Gladstone answered. There was a glimmer of excitement in his eyes, and I wondered if he might be on his way to recovery.

As Keefe shuffled past, he stopped and peered down his nose at me. "You think you got the upper hand today," he sneered. "Enjoy this feeling for now, because it's a false victory. In the Great Battle between Good and Evil as foretold in Revelations, *we will prevail.*"

"Oh, I'll enjoy this feeling, all right," I replied coolly. "And I hope *you* enjoy your prison cell."

Our plan had worked perfectly. As a result, we now had the evidence we needed to connect Keefe and his co-conspirators with the Project Abaddon plot.

While I was certainly thrilled, I couldn't help thinking of what Keefe had said to Gladstone just a few minutes before, about how I was "being taken care of."

What did he mean by that?

Chapter 26

With Jonah Keefe sitting in a jail cell in Concord, I spent all of Wednesday morning wracking my brain to figure out what I was missing in the hunt for the stolen Rembrandt for Peter Bowles.

I thought I knew exactly where the painting was hidden. But I needed a special key to be able to access it. My mind was so preoccupied by the question of where this key might be that I was surprised to find a postcard with a picture of the Kingdom of Light Church on it when I checked my mailbox shortly after lunch.

It was postmarked from Concord two days prior, and the handwritten message read:

> *I have information about the attack you prevented the other day. There's more to the plot than you might think. I'm taking an extreme risk in writing to you, but you need to know what I have to tell you. Meet me at the abandoned house on Mutton Road in Webster Wednesday night at 7 p.m. And come alone!*

The postcard was signed "Pam Arsenault," and it included a return address in Concord.

I checked the address for Pam Arsenault in the church directory, and it matched the return address written on the postcard. I also called the phone number listed for Pam in the directory, but I got her voice mail. I left a message saying I'd received her postcard and had a few questions about it—could she call me back as soon as she was able?

As five p.m. rolled around, and I hadn't heard back from Pam, I began to prepare for the mysterious meeting.

Of course, my first thought was that it was some kind of trap. I'm not an idiot, although I do admit to buying a Kid Rock CD back in the 1990s.

A clandestine meeting at an abandoned house in the middle of nowhere? That screamed "setup." But by whom? Jonah Keefe and his co-conspirators were all in jail.

And besides, I couldn't risk not finding out for myself. If the message *was* legitimate, perhaps there was a piece to the Project Abaddon puzzle that still remained unsolved—and I owed it to the city of Concord and the hundreds of potential victims to check it out.

Amalia was scheduled to work at the Tipsy Moose that evening. She'd already missed a few shifts at the bar to help me with my investigations, and I didn't want to impose on her any further by asking for backup in case it was a trap.

But I wasn't about to show up for the meeting unprepared, either. I made sure my cell phone was fully charged, and I took the canister of bear spray I carried on hikes in the woods. I also had the Swiss Army knife I brought with me everywhere, as well as a high-powered flashlight.

At five fifteen, I left my apartment and headed for Mutton Road in Webster. I got to the abandoned house shortly after six. I drove slowly past the house in the oncoming darkness, looking for potential danger.

The structure looked empty and eerily quiet, its windows boarded up, its roof sagging like a teenager's baggy jeans. As far as I could tell, there were no signs of anyone on the property.

I continued down the road and parked about a quarter of a mile away. I doubled back on foot and found a vantage point from which to watch the property in the woods across the street.

Around six thirty, a white Nissan Rogue slowed down as it approached the house. The car turned into the driveway and parked, and Pam Arsenault got out alone, carrying a flashlight. She walked up the front steps, opened the door, and went inside.

Through the cracks between the planks covering the windows, I saw a faint light emanating from inside the house. I watched and waited for another forty-five minutes, but I didn't see anyone else arrive.

Maybe Pam's message was sincere, I thought. *Maybe there was more to Project Abaddon after all.*

Satisfied that no one else was coming to ambush me, I emerged from my hiding place at quarter past seven and crossed the road to the house. I knocked softly on the front door and entered.

I was standing inside an empty living room, with a fireplace at the far end. Framing the fireplace mantel were built-in bookcases, their shelves obscured by cobwebs.

The light I'd seen from outside was coming from down the hall. I headed toward its source, calling out as I approached.

"Hello, Pam? It's me, Parker."

As I rounded a corner in the hallway, I found myself in what looked like a cavernous dining room. A large oak table was positioned in the center of the room, surrounded by six chairs. Perched on the middle of the table was a kerosene lantern, which was the source of the light. And seated at the head of the table, with her back toward me, was Pam Arsenault.

She didn't move or reply as I approached. And as I drew closer, I saw why.

She was leaning back in her chair, arms by her sides. Her mouth was open but her eyes were closed.

I tapped her lightly on the shoulder. When she didn't respond, I checked her neck for a pulse. Her heart was still beating, and she was breathing. But she was unconscious.

I noticed a rag on her lap. I picked it up to examine it, and the smell of chloroform made my eyes water.

I whirled around, looking for someone else in the room— and that's when I heard the front door slam shut.

* * *

A crackling noise that sounded like static interrupted the silence. Then, Livy Keefe's disembodied voice echoed throughout the house.

"Hello, Parker," she said icily. "You're a smart guy, so I assume you know why we've lured you here. Though, not so smart that you didn't fall for the trick."

Livy's voice was coming from a two-way radio transceiver lying on the table that I hadn't noticed before.

I picked up the handheld device and rushed to the front door, trying the handle.

Locked.

Looking more closely at the door handle, I realized the lockset had been switched out recently so that the door locked from the outside. Not only that, but unlocking it from the inside required a key code entered into a numeric keypad.

If it required a regular key, I could have picked the lock in seconds.

The postcard that brought me to the abandoned house was mailed two days earlier. That meant the scheme to ensnare me had been planned and put into motion before Jonah Keefe's arrest the night before. This must have been what Keefe was referring to when he told Gladstone I was being "taken care of."

I took out my cell phone and dialed 911, but the call couldn't be completed because I didn't have a signal. I texted Callie the address and the words "send help," but the text didn't go through, either.

Pressing the "transmit" button on the walkie-talkie, I asked Livy: "Were you involved in Project Abaddon from the start? Or are you just finishing your husband's business after I sent him to jail last night?"

I thought that tweaking Livy by reminding her I'd captured her husband would provoke anger. But instead, she cackled.

Her laughter crawled down the skin of my back like a scorpion.

"Was I involved? Sweetie, it was *my idea* to send those queers straight to Hell."

"If it was your idea, then how come you weren't at the meeting last night?"

While I kept Livy talking, I dashed through the rest of the house, searching for another way out.

"Some of those men aren't so enlightened. They think a woman's job is to shut up and have babies. Jonah and I thought it would be better if I stayed in the shadows."

Sure, makes sense. Not everyone is as enlightened as you.

All of the windows in the house were boarded up. The only

door was the front door that locked from the outside.

"Was Pam Arsenault part of the plot?"

"No. That bitch is just collateral damage." Livy sounded out of breath, and I heard sloshing noises in the background.

"She told me you resented her because she called you out for copying her crocheted items for the church fair."

"What did she think [*slosh*], that she had a copyright on any kind of crocheted creatures? [*slosh*] She's a fool."

The house had a basement with a bulkhead, but the bulkhead doors were chained shut.

"How did you get Pam to help lure me?"

"I wrote that postcard inviting you here, and I asked Pam to meet me here at six thirty to talk about how I might leave Jonah safely," she said proudly. "I thought you might not be as suspicious if you saw her car in the driveway."

The smell of gasoline bludgeoned my nostrils.

"You must have gotten here pretty early yourself. I was watching the house from six o'clock on."

"That's right," Livy crowed. "I was here at five."

She continued to hold down the "transmit" button, and the sound of a butane lighter sparking into flame punctured my lungs like an icicle.

"Goodbye, Parker," she intoned. "I'm done answering your questions. Consider this a little preview of what your soul will endure for all eternity."

She signed off: "May you burn in Hell forever like the sinner you are."

Chapter 27

The house was built decades ago, and it quickly went up in flames—its wooden clapboards snapping and popping from the rapidly spreading fire.

The heat hit me instantly. I felt like a turkey roasting in an oven.

I grabbed a chair from the dining room and hurried to the nearest window. I slammed the chair against the window, the glass shattering. But the chair broke apart in my hands when it struck the sturdy boards nailed across the window's opening.

I sprinted to the front door and tried some basic numeric combinations on the electronic lock: 1111, 2222, 3333…

As the door remained locked and I realized I wasn't getting anywhere, I stepped back and delivered a ferocious kick where the latch met the jamb. But as old as the house was, the door jamb held. I wasn't nearly strong enough to smash it open.

The heat felt like thousands of tiny needles pricking my skin. Smoke also began to fill the house, and I covered my nose and mouth with my shirt as I choked on the fumes.

Dropping to the floor to escape the worst of the smoke, I scuttled through the house looking for some kind of tool that could give me the leverage I needed to break open the door or a window. But aside from the table and chairs in the dining room, the house was empty.

As I passed through the dining room again, I pulled Pam Arsenault's body from the chair and laid it out on the floor to minimize the risk of damage from the smoke.

My skin was screaming by this point. I tried to visualize plunging my body into an ice bath to manage the pain. But my head felt woozy from all the smoke. I slumped to the floor and sprawled out next to Pam, unable to move.

Summoning every shot of energy I had left, I brought my phone close to my face, imploring the device to show a bar or two indicating a signal. But through the hazy tears in my eyes, I saw that the words "no signal" remained on the screen.

My arm dropped like a sandbag from an old movie set, my hand still desperately clutching the phone. I shut my eyes and tried to block out the pain.

Amid the roar of the flames, I heard loud crashing sounds that I assumed were chunks of the house collapsing around me. I imagined that I was floating off the floor, airborne, carried by some unseen force away from the light and the heat and toward darkness and emptiness and extinction.

* * *

When I opened my eyes again, I was staring up at the face of a female firefighter.

"We're going to roll you over now," she murmured, "so we can slide a stretcher underneath you."

I was lying on the grass some fifty yards from the abandoned house. My clothes were singed and sooty, and an oxygen mask was strapped over my face. My entire body stung, like nettles had burrowed underneath my skin.

I looked to my right. I could see that the house was still ablaze, but most of the fire was out. A half dozen firefighters were wielding hoses, with streams of water jetting from the nozzles and dousing the remaining flames. The house's burnt-out husk rose from its foundation like a specter, a thick plume of smoke billowing from the lifeless structure.

I looked to my left. Pam Arsenault was already lying on a stretcher, and two firefighters lifted her off the ground and carried to her a waiting ambulance. She was still unconscious, but she was wearing an oxygen mask as well, and she appeared to be breathing.

At least, the blanket that covered her body didn't extend over her face.

"Thank you for getting us out of the building," I croaked. My throat felt dry and scratchy from inhaling so much smoke.

"That wasn't us," the woman said, her face illuminated in a reddish glow every few seconds as the lights from the firetrucks rotated. "You were already lying here on the ground when we arrived."

I felt two pairs of hands lift up the left side of my body and then gently set me down on a stretcher.

As I was being hoisted off the ground and carried to the ambulance, I glanced back—and I noticed pistachio shells scattered on the ground next to where I had lain.

* * *

I spent the night in the intensive care unit at the hospital. Kris and Amalia took care of Minerva, and Callie stayed with me in my hospital room.

I had first or second degree burns over much of my body. But the doctors said I was lucky not to have suffered from third degree burns. Although I'd be in pain, I would make a full and speedy recovery.

Pam Arsenault faced a similar situation. I was allowed to

leave the hospital late on Thursday afternoon, my blistered skin covered in ointment and wrapped in bandages. Because Pam had been unconscious for so long, they kept her at the hospital one more night for observation.

I texted Detective Connor from my hospital bed on Thursday morning. Later that morning, he arrested Livy Keefe at her home. Livy was charged with two counts of attempted murder for the offenses against Pam and me, as well as conspiracy to commit murder for her role in Project Abaddon.

Connor later told me that when he'd read the charges against her, Livy shot back: "You have no proof that I was part of that conspiracy!"

In response to her outburst, he calmly played the audio file I'd sent him along with my text. It was a recording of the entire conversation I'd had with Livy over the two-way radios the night before.

As soon as I'd heard Livy's voice in the abandoned house, I'd had the presence of mind to activate the audio recording app on my phone. Although I wasn't able to pick up a cellular signal, I was still able to use one of the most powerful pieces of technology in an investigator's modern arsenal to ensure that Livy would face justice for her crimes.

* * *

Callie brought me home from the hospital on Thursday afternoon, and she called out of work to take care of me that evening.

"I haven't been completely honest with you," I told her as she cooked us a dinner of stir-fried vegetables over rice. "I'd like to come clean."

"Oh, God. Don't tell me you're seeing someone else."

"No, it's nothing like that. But you deserve to know what

kind of dangers I face in my career. And if you decide you don't want to be here to pick up the pieces every time I get into trouble, I wouldn't blame you if you left."

I told her all about my encounters with Todd Primo, including the deal I'd made with him to learn who the shooter was in the Project Abaddon plot—and also that I believed it was one of his henchmen who'd saved Pam and me from the fire the night before.

"So they've been following you this whole time?" she asked, clearly shaken.

"That's what I suspect, yes."

"Why would this guy Spiller risk his life to save you from a burning building?"

"He probably figured if he kept me alive, I might eventually lead him to that missing Rembrandt."

"Why didn't you ask Amalia to go with you to that abandoned house?" she queried. "Especially if you thought it was a trap."

"She was working, and I didn't want to impose. Besides, she was supposed to save me from a mob boss, not the Church Lady."

We ate our dinner in silence. As I gave Callie the space to process what I'd told her, I thought about what she'd said with regard to Amalia.

My work was becoming increasingly dangerous, and maybe I did need Amalia around all the time. Perhaps I should ask her if she wanted a full-time job?

When we finished eating, Callie took our plates, rinsed them off, and put them in the dishwasher. Then she came to me and kissed me gently on the top of my head—one of the few areas of my body that didn't hurt.

"Thank you for trusting me with the information about Todd

Primo," she said. "I wish you'd told me sooner, but I understand you were only trying to protect me. I need you to know that I want you in my life—and if that means picking up the pieces when there's trouble, then that's what I'll do. But you have to do the same for me in return."

"Of course."

"I'm serious. If I sprain an ankle while dancing, I want you to take care of me. If my students lose a tough competition, I expect you to be there to console me. And," she added wryly, "if I ever have an organized crime lord's henchmen following *me* around, maybe pressuring me to throw a high-stakes dance comp they've got big money riding on, I'll be sure to share that burden with *you* as well."

* * *

We spent the rest of the evening discussing Bowles's case and where the key to the Rembrandt that I strongly suspected was stashed in the cabin on Beth Lane in Meredith might be.

"In the Project Abaddon case, so many people weren't who they appeared to be," I noted. "Trace Gladstone seemed like a good candidate for the shooter, but he had nothing to do with the plot. Livy Keefe seemed harmless, but she ended up being the mastermind. And even in this case, the same idea applies. We thought the phrase *Beth/Meredith* in Walter Cobb's journal referred to people, when it was actually a place. We thought *Romeo Hotel, Lima* was a place, but it was actually a person. Maybe we're looking at the rest of the journal entry all wrong as well."

"Does the date *November 15* refer to the year 1990, just a few months after that August twenty-seventh journal entry?" Callie asked. "Did you look in the journal for an entry on that date?"

"I did. There was no journal entry on November fifteenth. The next one came on December twelfth."

"And what theories have you tried about the meaning of the letter 'C'?"

"At first I thought it was a musical key. But the keyhole in the fireplace mantel of Cobb's cabin doesn't suggest this. It looks like it requires something more like a traditional key, though it's not a lock I can pick—it's in the shape of a diamond. As for other theories, I've tried everything the letter 'C' might stand for, including carbon, Celsius, and even the 'C' programming language. I've been thinking about this question almost without a break for days now."

"Wait a minute. Let me see that journal entry again," Callie said.

I handed her the photocopy of the journal page.

"When you said *without a break* just now, it made me wonder: What if the line break after '*Key of C.*' is random, and not indicative of a sentence break?"

My jaw dropped like a trap door in a magician's act. "You mean, those final two lines might actually be one sentence? *Key in C. Corner lot, November 15?*"

Callie whipped out her phone and searched online.

"Bingo." She handed me her phone with a euphoric smile.

I was looking at a web page for a long-term parking lot in Meredith called the Cozy Corner.

Cozy Corner lot. Or … *C. Corner lot.*

"Callie, you're a genius!" I blurted.

"Beauty *and* brains," she replied with a flourish.

Chapter 28

With the chance to find a missing masterpiece at stake, Callie, Amalia, and Kris all called out of work the next morning.

The choice was simple: Punch a clock—or make history?

Todd Primo's henchman saving my life two days earlier was a blunt reminder that I was constantly being tailed—and that Primo would do anything to seize the painting if he were able. With this thought in mind, we took elaborate measures to ensure we weren't being followed.

At ten a.m., Callie drove me to a local store. We entered the store through the front door and snuck out through the back exit, leaving Callie's car in the parking lot. Amalia and Kris were waiting in a back alley in Kris's car. Callie and I climbed inside and laid down on the back seat until we were on Route 293 heading north toward Meredith.

An hour later, we were cruising into the Cozy Corner parking lot. Callie and I went to talk to the lot manager, while Kris and Amalia stayed in the car.

The manager was a young guy who looked like a cartoon bouncer. He had broad shoulders and huge, beefy arms, but a tiny waist and twigs for legs.

I showed the manager my PI license. "Do you have someone

named either Walter Cobb or Ty Wobblecart renting a space in your lot?"

"You got a warrant?" he challenged.

"No, but what I *do* have is an opportunity. We're about this close to finding a multimillion-dollar painting," I said, holding my fingers a few millimeters apart. "When we do—thanks to the information you're about to give us—there will be a media frenzy. And we'll be sure to thank your business for helping to make it happen."

"Nope. I'm not buying it," he said. "Come back with a warrant and we'll talk."

As Callie and I left his office, I shook my head. "What was so hard to believe about that story?"

"Ironically," she replied, "every word was true."

* * *

"No dice," I said when we got back to Kris's car. "But let's take a look around, see what we can find for ourselves."

We walked around the lot, unsure of what we were looking for.

"Hey, didn't you say something about November 15?" Amalia called out. She was looking down at the pavement.

"Yeah. Why?"

"The sections of the lot seem to be identified by letters. We're in section 'K' right now."

"So?"

"So, November is the signifier for the letter 'N' in the NATO Phonetic Alphabet."

"Oh my God, Amalia, you're right!" Cobb had already used the NATO alphabet earlier in his journal entry. It seemed so obvious in hindsight.

We scattered throughout the lot, searching for section "N."

"Over here!" Kris cried.

The space numbered N15 held what my dad would generously call a "beater car"—something you don't worry about beating on, because it's only a few miles from the junkyard anyway. It was a black Subaru Legacy, with scratches on the quarter panels and rust spots on the doors.

The doors were locked, and though I knew how to pick the locks on building doors, opening locked car doors was a different skill set that was not in my wheelhouse.

"In for a penny," Amalia said. She used her elbow to break the glass in the passenger's side door window, then reached in and unlocked the car's doors.

"What if this isn't Cobb's car?" I said, realizing I was echoing what Amalia had said to me when we broke into Cobb's cabin and that our roles were now reversed.

"Look at this car," she countered. "It can't be worth much. If the driver files an insurance claim, they'll probably get back more for the broken window than the car itself is worth."

"Okay, look for a key in the shape of a diamond," I said as we all piled into the Subaru.

"Found it!" Kris said about thirty seconds later. She held up a well-worn silver device that looked like it belonged in a toolbox. "It was in the center console box."

"Holy shit," Callie said, looking at each of us in turn. "Are we actually going to do this?"

* * *

We arrived at Walter Cobb's cabin on Lake Waukewan shortly after noon. I picked the lock again, and the four of us shuffled inside, our nerves like guitar strings that had been stretched too tight, mere seconds from snapping.

The air around us felt charged, like the moment before

lightning strikes.

Callie drew in her breath at the beauty of the cabin and its natural setting. "This is the kind of place I'd love to live in some day," she gaped.

We approached the fireplace as if it were some kind of magical talisman, like Indiana Jones as he's about to take possession of the Golden Idol in the opening sequence of the movie *Raiders of the Lost Ark*—and I smiled at the recollection that Callie had jokingly compared me to Dr. Jones just a few weeks before.

Holding my breath in anticipation, I inserted the key into the diamond-shaped hole in the mantel and gently turned it.

Slowly, the inset panel in the chimney's facade began to slide upward, and I heard Callie gasp.

There, above the mantel in front of us, was *A Lady and Gentleman in Black*. A nearly four-hundred-year-old painting that only a handful of people in the world had seen in the last thirty-five years.

"It's mesmerizing," Kris whispered.

As we gazed at the painting in awe, I remembered something I'd read about it while researching the Gardner Museum heist.

During an X-ray examination of the work, it was discovered that Rembrandt had originally painted the image of a child along with the couple, but later he'd painted over it. Art historians believe the child had died between the time the painting was commissioned and when the work was finished, and the couple had asked Rembrandt to remove the child from the painting so as not to stir up painful memories.

Seeing the painting up close and in person, it struck me that Rembrandt had subtly yet ingeniously captured the couple's grief. To anyone who didn't know the painting's back story, this grief might not be immediately obvious. But when you knew the whole context, their tragic loss became hauntingly evident in the tautness of the couple's features and the vacant look in their eyes.

And suddenly I realized why Cobb had been so drawn to this painting—and why he'd added it to his personal collection, despite the fact that it was stolen property.

Cynthia Forrest had mentioned that her uncle had also lost a child. He must have felt a poignant kinship with the painting's subjects.

I imagined Cobb sitting by himself in this secret cottage by the lake, staring for hours at the painting, his eyes naturally drawn to the empty space where the ill-fated child had been leaning against its mother's knee.

In Christopher Marlow's sixteenth century play *The Tragical History of Doctor Faustus*, based on the German myth of Faust, the demon Mephistopheles says: *"Solamen miseris socios habuisse doloris,"* which roughly translates to "It is a comfort to the unfortunate to have had companions in woe."

Or, to put it another way: *Misery loves company*.

Ms. Forrest and the other people I'd spoken with about Walter Cobb had described him as a serious, even mirthless person who was somewhat of a loner. Maybe owning *A Lady and Gentleman in Black* was Cobb's way of seeking community.

In feeling an unspoken connection with the grieving couple in the painting, Cobb was probably able to feel a little bit less desolate himself.

Chapter 29

Needless to say, the executives at the Gardner Museum were overjoyed to get one of their stolen paintings back.

Not wanting to risk any further damage to the work in trying to remove it, I immediately called Lauren Toews and told her about our discovery. She arrived a few hours later with a crew of preservationists to retrieve it.

I also called Peter Bowles and Cynthia Forrest, and they joined us on the lake as well. Aside from her delight at recovering the missing painting, Cynthia was also very grateful to learn about this secret waterfront dwelling that made her feel closer to her uncle.

Kris drove back into town to buy champaign, brandy, and other spirits, and we all celebrated at the cottage late into the night.

The museum had set a reward of $10 million for information that led to the return of all thirteen stolen items. Because this was the first of the missing objects to be returned, they offered us $1 million from this reward money, of which my share was $160,000.

Bowles very generously included the value of the cottage in his assessment of my fee, and so I was pleasantly surprised to get a check for more than $300,000 from him a week later. Not a bad haul for just under a month's work.

I invested the money right away. I planned to use it to help more people who couldn't afford my services. Assuming an annual five-percent rate of return, I could keep the principle intact and use the interest to provide about $15,000 worth of *pro bono* work for clients each year.

I wasn't crazy about all the publicity I received for finding the stolen Rembrandt. But as Callie reminded me, it was good for business.

The story was international news for a full week, and I had media requests for interviews from as far away as New Zealand. As a former journalist, I could appreciate their need for content—and I felt bad about not being able to accommodate them all. But I had to look out for my own well-being, and I was pretty far out of my comfort zone being on the other side of a microphone.

I made appearances on *The View*, *The Today Show*, and *The Drew Barrymore Show*. But I wanted to give equal time to nontraditional media outlets, so I also sat in as a guest on some true crime and topical news podcasts.

Oh, and I took Callie shopping for a high-end gown as well— just in case we were invited to next year's Met Gala.

* * *

Eleven days after discovering the missing Rembrandt, Callie and I were seated in a ballroom at The Hotel Concord, tensely awaiting the results of the election along with Lionel Hartman's campaign staff, friends and family, and major donors.

A jazz trio was playing on a stage in the corner of the room. Callie looked stunning in a midnight blue dress, her hair done up in a French twist. I managed not to embarrass myself in a cobalt-colored suit without a tie.

The returns had been trickling in all evening, and they showed that Gordon and Hartman were in a virtual dead heat in the race for governor.

"Just watching Alex is making me more nervous than I already am," Callie said.

She was referring to Alexandria Lawson, Hartman's campaign manager, who hadn't sat down all evening. A slight, thirty-something woman with short blond hair and a friendly smile that masked a ferocious intensity, Lawson was hustling around the room, talking into a Bluetooth headset and maintaining an up-to-the-minute tally of results from the state's various precincts on the iPad she carried with her everywhere.

"I suppose keeping busy is how she deals with the stress of the evening," I replied.

My own coping strategy involved glancing every few minutes at my phone, following the Bruins as they battled the Seattle Kraken on a West Coast road trip. Seattle played a smashmouth brand of hockey, and their physical style was making it hard for the B's to generate any high-quality chances in a scoreless first period.

Callie and I had gotten to know Alex as we'd become more involved in Hartman's campaign in recent days.

In fact, when Alex learned that I'd been a political reporter for the *Concord Herald* for many years, she'd asked for my input in shaping Hartman's closing argument to the voters. I'd written the draft of a speech that I'd run by them both.

I could have focused on Gordon's considerable corruption, like his administration's bid rigging scheme and ties to a gun smuggling operation. Instead, inspired by my recent thoughts about the nature of community, I chose to emphasize Hartman's natural empathy for others and his inclusive approach to building a shared society that works for everyone.

We all have many communities we belong to. These may be defined by the school or college we attended, our place of employment, our clubs and activities, our chosen profession, our religious or political affiliation, our sports fandom, our ethnicity, and our city, state, and country of residency, to name some examples.

But there's a natural hierarchy to these communities. This is why state laws take priority over local town ordinances, and national laws supersede state laws. And before we're members of a church or political party, before we're even citizens of any country or territory, we're human beings first. Therefore, our ultimate allegiance should be to our shared humanity.

When a society is defined by factional communities in constant conflict with each other, it can't function effectively. We've become so focused on our identities within these smaller, tribal communities that we've lost sight of the fact that we're part of a larger society. We've forgotten how to coexist, how to be kind to one another and work together for a better future.

This was the message I wanted Hartman to leave the voters with. This was the vision I wanted to carve out for his administration: that Hartman would build an inclusive society where everyone mattered and that the government would balance the needs and interests of everyone equally, rather than catering to a few smaller, exclusive communities—like the rich, or members of its own party, or certain races or religions.

Hartman had loved the speech, and he'd given it several times as he traversed the state while making his final pitch to voters. Now, as we waited for the results to be announced, I felt like the entire election was a referendum on this view of community.

As I refreshed the browser on my phone screen to get another update on the Bruins game, it occurred to me that hockey was a good example of what I was referring to. Perhaps that was another reason why I loved the sport so much.

There are thirty-two teams in the National Hockey League. Each team can be seen as its own tribal community. Yet, the sport itself is like one big brotherhood. Yes, there are rivalries—and even some bad blood once in a while. But for the most part, players look out for each other. Maybe because it's a dangerous sport, with the possibility for serious injury every time you're out on the ice.

Hockey is also the only professional sport in which the players from both teams line up, shake hands, and congratulate each other after the championship has been decided. Hockey embodies what a healthy society should be, with everyone connected by a thread of mutual respect and local differences set aside for the greater good.

"Hey, something's happening," Callie said, interrupting my internal musing.

She pointed to Alex, who was scampering over to the table where Hartman sat with his wife and some high-rolling campaign donors.

Alex whispered something into Hartman's ear, and I couldn't tell from his reaction whether it was good or bad news.

Hartman was another person I didn't want to play cards with, I realized.

As Hartman leaned over and whispered to his wife, Alex strode over to the podium that was set up on a dais at the front of the ballroom, where Hartman would be giving either a victory or a concession speech later that night.

"Ladies and gentlemen, if I could have your attention for just a minute…" Alex said.

The band stopped playing, and the room grew silent except for a single cough. All eyes were focused on Alex.

"I've just learned that CNN is about to call the New Hampshire governor's race on air. Will everyone please join me in congratulating the Granite State's next leader, Governor-elect Lionel Hartman!"

The ballroom erupted in bedlam.

Callie squealed with delight, and I let out a loud whoop. We embraced and kissed as a cargo net stretched across the ceiling was released and white balloons cascaded down around us.

Confetti was shot from miniature cannons, and the band launched into a jaunty tune. The red, white, and blue confetti dusted the revelers' heads and shoulders like a newly fallen snow that was soon to arrive in that part of the country, and I felt sorry for the workers who had to clean up in the morning.

"Wanna dance?" Callie asked. Her eyes shimmered with an unspoken invitation, playful and tender all at once—and in that moment, I realized I wanted to dance all of my dances with her for the rest of eternity.

"Sure. But you're a professional, and I wouldn't even call myself an amateur."

"That's okay. I'm an exceptional teacher."

I felt my phone vibrate, interrupting the moment. Against my better judgment, I looked at the screen to see who was calling.

Todd Primo.

"Hold that thought," I told Callie, and I answered the call.

"Parker! Congratulations on your friend Lionel Hartman winning the governor's race."

"He's not my friend. He barely knows me."

"Yes, but he knows *of* you. Listen, I hate to spoil your celebration, but we need to talk. It's urgent. Why don't you tell Callie that you have to step out for a few minutes? I won't keep you long, and then you can get back to the party. Rico and Spiller are downstairs in the lobby waiting for you."

My blood felt thin and cold, like ice cracking underfoot.

Primo not only knew exactly where I was at that moment. *He also knew Callie by name.*

"I'll be right down."

* * *

Rico and Spiller escorted me wordlessly to a black Cadillac Escalade parked around the corner from the hotel.

I suppose I should have thanked Spiller for saving my life. But at that moment, I wasn't sure how grateful I was.

Rico opened the car's rear door for me. I climbed into the back seat next to Primo, who greeted me with a nod. Nick the Neck sat behind the wheel.

"Do you recognize this voice?" Primo asked. He took out his cell phone, tapped the screen, and held the phone up for me to listen.

I heard my own voice coming through the phone's speaker. *"You've been in contact with a South African courier about purchasing some stolen diamonds. What you don't know is that the courier is an FBI agent, and the deal is a sting operation."*

I closed my eyes and sighed.

Primo had recorded our conversation in the Concord Library. Just like I'd recorded Livy Keefe the following week.

"What do you want from me?" I said, opening my eyes again.

Primo's face was obscured in shadow, so I had no image to go with his words. All I had were the words themselves. Falling out of the darkness, cold and hard, like hailstones in an overnight storm.

"Nothing, for the moment. But your proximity to our new governor makes you a valuable asset. Someday I'm going to ask you for a favor, and I'd appreciate your cooperation. If you do what I ask, then no one ever has to hear this recording. Do we understand each other?"

"We do."

Primo rapped on the window beside him, and Rico opened my door. I got out of the car and returned to the hotel alone.

Like a hockey goalie paid to throw a game, I was ethically compromised. Like Minerva on her leash, I was controlled by someone else.

As I walked back to the hotel, I had Nirvana's version of that David Bowie song stuck in my head from hearing it the other day. The wind had picked up in intensity, and the weather had turned frigid as the calendar advanced to November.

I turned up my collar, gazed a gazeless stare, and thought about how *I* was the man who'd sold the world.

Or, at least my soul.

Notes

Thanks for reading my book. Your support means a lot to me.

If you enjoyed what you read, I'd appreciate it if you could leave a short review on Amazon or Goodreads. It doesn't have to be long; one or two sentences on what you liked the most about the book and why is enough. Reviews like this are critical in supporting independent authors and helping other readers find stories they like.

Please also tell your friends and family members about this book, and anyone else you know who likes to read mysteries. Word-of-mouth marketing is critical for independent authors who don't have a large platform for reaching potential readers.

I have one more request as well. If you liked this book, please sign up for my mailing list, where you'll get sneak peeks and updates on my works in progress, as well as other exclusive content. I promise I won't overwhelm you with messages— once a month is all you'll hear from me—and in return for signing up, you'll also get a *free* collection of my short stories.

You can sign up for my mailing list on my author website: **denniswpierce.com**.

If you keep reading, you'll find a preview of the next book in the Parker Hanson Mystery series, *Full Court Press*, in another page or two. In this third installment in the series, Parker and Amalia face their toughest challenges yet as they investigate a web of legal corruption at the request of Callie's father—while also contending with a pair of old enemies.

But first, I'd like to share some notes about the book you just finished reading and acknowledge those whose help was instrumental in bringing it to life.

While the events depicted in this work are fictional, much of the information they're based on is real.

For instance, there is no Leone crime family that I'm aware of, and the notion that one of the missing Rembrandts ended up in the hands of a collector is purely a result of my imagination. But the other details about the Gardner Museum heist are true—and as of this book's publication, the largest unsolved art theft in history has continued to baffle investigators.

If you'd like to learn more about the crime itself, one of the sources I relied on for my research was Shelley Murphy's excellent story in the *Boston Globe*: "On the 35th anniversary of the Gardner Museum heist, retired FBI agent offers theory on whodunnit" (March 18, 2025).

Similarly, the information about LGBTQ+ History Month is accurate, as are the highlights from LGBTQ+ history within the Granite State, which I learned from various sources online. While other New Hampshire communities have honored LGBTQ+ History Month with public celebrations, including the city of Keene, I'm not aware of any such events having taken place in Concord before.

Once again, I'd like to thank former U.S. Army Captain Tom LaBelle for his insight into how a Ranger and a SEAL might interact. I'd also like to thank my entire family for their love and support—especially my mom, Fran, for passing along her passion for reading to me at a very young age; my wife, Jean, for her steadfast encouragement; and my daughters, Elise and Gabrielle, for their social media marketing savvy. I love you all so much.

And now, here's the first chapter of the next book in the Parker Hanson Mystery series, *Full Court Press...*

* * *

The Boston Celtics were letting me down.

I was sitting in a luxury suite at the TD Garden with my girlfriend, Callie Stewart. We were watching the Celtics play the Atlanta Hawks during a Thursday night NBA game in early February.

"Hey, I see Donnie Wahlberg sitting courtside," Callie said, pointing to the Boston-based actor and former musician.

"Is he hangin' tough?" I asked.

"You got it."

I had never been inside a luxury suite before. In fact, I'd only been to the Garden a handful of times, sitting way up in the nosebleed seats to watch the Bruins play hockey.

The tickets were given to us by Callie's father, Rory. He was a lawyer for a high-powered firm in Concord, New Hampshire.

The firm leased a luxury suite to entertain clients at home Celtics games. But I wasn't a client myself. Actually, the law firm was a client of *mine*. Rory had hired me to look into questionable practices within the New Hampshire state court system, and he'd given Callie and me the tickets as a gesture of gratitude for taking the case.

Callie was having a great time. But I was stewing. The Celtics were playing uninspired basketball, and they were losing badly in the third quarter, 80 to 62.

"That's some stellar choreography," Callie said, nodding toward the Celtics Dancers as they performed a routine for the crowd during a TV timeout. "I think I might have to borrow some of those moves for our recital this spring." Callie was a dance instructor for school-age students at a studio in Concord.

I suppose I should have been enjoying myself regardless of the game's score. After all, the food in the suite was exquisite: shrimp cocktail, oysters, Caesar salad, beef tenderloin, and cheesecake.

And so was the company, as Callie and I had the entire suite to ourselves.

I had been thinking lately about asking Callie to marry me. I was as sure as the streets in Boston were crooked and confusing that I wanted to wake up next to her every morning for the rest of my life. But we'd only been dating for seven months, and I didn't want to scare her off by asking her too soon. I was also trying to figure out just how to pop the question.

When you're sharing an evening in a private luxury suite with the person you want as your life partner, that should be enough to foster contentment. Yet, it bothered me that the Celtics merely seemed to be going through the motions in the game.

I was more of a baseball and hockey fan by nature. But the Bruins were struggling this year, and the Celtics were having a highly successful season. So I'd switched up my viewing habits that winter.

For the last few months, the C's were all I really had to look forward to. And by "C's," I meant the Celtics—and Callie.

Following basketball was a welcome reprieve from worrying about my obligation to a mob boss, Todd Primo, who was blackmailing me into doing some future favor for him. Frankly, I wished he would just get it over with and ask for my help already. Having that debt looming over me was taking an angle grinder to my nerves.

Watching b-ball also kept me from thinking about a threat I'd recently gotten from former New Hampshire Governor Jack Gordon. I'd arrived home at my Manchester apartment the other day to find a note taped to my front door, with a handwritten message scrawled in black ink. The message was short but not at all sweet:

I'm coming for you.

At least, I assumed the note was from Gordon. I'd broken up a gun smuggling ring that I suspected Gordon had been a part of back in July. Although I wasn't able to prove Gordon's involvement, I'd campaigned on behalf of his opponent, Lionel Hartman, in the election that fall, and Hartman had won. That gave Gordon two good reasons to want me dead.

Yet, I guess the threat could have come from someone connected with the New Hampshire Supreme Court system instead. Callie's father believed that at least one, and maybe more, of the court's five justices were accepting bribes to influence the outcome of key rulings. I'd only recently started investigating, but maybe I was already stirring up trouble.

So, yeah—basketball served as an entertaining diversion from these more pressing concerns, and lately that escape had been working. The Celtics were playing crisp, unselfish, fundamentally sound hoops—sharing the rock, not getting bogged down in "iso" ball—the way the game was meant to be played. Coming into the Hawks game, they were on a major hot streak.

Which made that evening's contest all the more maddening.

It was the first time I'd ever seen them play live, and they seemed to be sleepwalking through much of the game.

It's funny how much a sports fan's mood rises and falls along with their team's fortunes. For the players, it's just another game, one of eighty-two spread across a grueling, eight-month season. For us fans, though, it's much more than that. Especially if you're shelling out big bucks for parking and souvenirs—even if the tickets themselves were free.

With three minutes left in the third quarter, Celtics point guard Derrick White drove into the lane and passed the ball out to shooting guard Jaylen Brown. But Brown wasn't paying attention, and the ball skittered out of bounds for another careless turnover.

Celtics coach Joe Mazzulla called a timeout as boos rained down from the stands.

Callie was saying something to me, but between the music blaring during the stoppage of play and the noise from the crowd, I couldn't hear her.

"Sorry," I said, pointing to my ear. "It's so loud right now."

"In sports arenas," she said, riffing on the famous tagline for the movie *Alien*, "no one can hear you scream."

I laughed and then gestured toward the spread behind us.

"Want anything from the buffet?"

"I'm all set, thanks."

As I was helping myself to more shrimp and Caesar salad, there was knock on the door to our suite. The door opened, and a TD Garden attendant poked his head into the room.

"Excuse me, sir. Are you Parker Hanson?"

"In the flesh."

"There's a call for you. If you'll follow me, I can show you to the phone."

I wondered who would be trying to reach me at the TD Garden that evening. Callie's father knew we were at the game, obviously. But he would have dialed my cell phone. Maybe it was someone else from the firm who didn't have my direct number.

"I'll be right back," I told Callie.

I followed the attendant down the hall. We walked halfway around the concourse to the other side of the arena, where he pointed into a small room and said, "In here, sir."

There was a desk with a phone on it inside the room, and one of the buttons on the phone was flashing. I picked up the receiver, pressed the flashing button, and said, "Hello? This is Parker Hanson speaking."

I was met with silence on the other end of the line.

I turned around to talk with the attendant. But he had disappeared.

An uneasy feeling crept into my chest like a crocodile searching for prey. I called Callie's cell phone, but the call went right to voice mail.

I hurried back to our suite. When I got there, the door was ajar.

I pushed it open and saw that the room was in disarray: The chairs we'd been sitting in were overturned. The seafood tower had toppled, and shrimp and oysters were scattered around the floor. Cheesecake was smeared across the buffet table.

Suddenly, I had much bigger problems to worry about than an eighteen-point deficit heading into the fourth quarter of the game.

Callie was gone.

www.ingramcontent.com/pod-product-compliance
Lightning Source LLC
Chambersburg PA
CBHW011323310726
48973CB00011B/3033